SHIRLEY ALLEN

TO LOVE
IN VAIN

Complete and Unabridged

LINFORD
Leicester

First published in Great Britain in 1996

First Linford Edition
published 1999

British Library CIP Data

Allen, Shirley
    To love in vain.—Large print ed.—
Linford romance library
    1. Love stories
    2. Large type books
    I. Title
    823.9'14 [F]

ISBN 0–7089–5406–5

Published by
F. A. Thorpe (Publishing) Ltd.
Anstey, Leicestershire

Set by Words & Graphics Ltd.
Anstey, Leicestershire
Printed and bound in Great Britain by
T. J. International Ltd., Padstow, Cornwall

This book is printed on acid-free paper

TO LOVE IN VAIN

When her father dies in a duel, Anna has no money to pay off his debts and is thrown into Newgate Gaol. However, she is freed by her cousin Julien, who takes her to her grandparents in France. Finding herself surrounded by people she cannot trust, Anna turns more and more to the handsome, caring Patrick St. Clair. Then, to her horror, she discovers her guardians are planning her marriage to a man of their choosing!

Books by Shirley Allen
in the Linford Romance Library:

RACE FOR LOVE

1

Anna opened her eyes wearily, immediately aware of the pain in her right leg where the wound was festering. Still worse than the pain was the indescribable filth and squalor of her surroundings, for this was Newgate prison, in the year Seventeen hundred and eighty-eight, and no place for animals, let alone the ill, pathetic people who were housed here.

'You awake, Anna?' Meg Skeels asked. The woman was sitting hunched in a corner next to her. 'How's that leg of yours doing?'

Anna smiled at her friend of the past few weeks.

'Better now that the fetters are off! It was very kind of you to pay to have that done for me, and the bandage you've put on my leg has helped a lot, too.'

'Won't do it much good stuck

in here, though.' The older woman mused, ruefully. 'The way things are going it could be a long while before it starts to improve and be prepared for it to get worse before it gets better.'

Anna shuddered, and wondered for the thousandth time how she'd come to be incarcerated in this living hell.

To her, the past weeks were a blur of unreality, for one moment she had been the feted daughter of Henry Heatherington, and then, on her father's sudden death in a duel, she had been transported to Newgate in his stead.

Henry Heatherington had been hopelessly in debt, and may well have stooped to the practice of highway robbery in a vain attempt to replenish a family fortune which had been extinguished due to his passion for gambling.

Even so, Anna might have escaped the final ignominy of Newgate if it hadn't been for the malevolence of Lady Weathercombe, who had previously been anxious to seek Anna's hand in marriage for her puny, weakling son.

Anger at having played hostess to a penniless girl with a rogue for a father, had caused her to vent her frustrations on the unfortunate Anna.

'Meg, how long do you think they'll keep us here?' Anna asked the older woman who had taken her under her wing.

'I don't rightly know, dearie. Till the Assizes sit, I should think. But there's not much point in being in a hurry, after all, t'will be a choice of the rope or transportation, most like, and which of them is best? Well, that's Hobson's choice!'

'But you,' Meg continued, 'you could well have a choice! I've a feeling that Black Will is quite taken with you. Now, if you was to be nice to him, well, he might well find a way of getting you out of here!'

'Black Will! That great, hulking

brute! Oh, Meg, surely you can't be serious?'

'Aye, well I know that our gaoler's no oil painting and he can have a filthy temper, too, if you muck him around, but I tell you, girl, if I was pleasing to the eye like you are, I'd not hesitate!'

She laughed raucously, waking up some of the other women, so that there were groans and cries of 'Shout your mouth, Meg Skeels, some of us are trying to sleep here!'

' 'Tis morning now, you lazy doxies! Anyway, I wasn't speaking to you lot, I was speaking to my friend here!'

'Well keep your voice down, then!' Lizzie Lane croaked. She was consumptive, and unlikely to survive much longer in the cold, fetid conditions of Newgate . . .

'All right, Liz. For you I will!' Meg agreed, compassion in her voice, and when she spoke next, her voice was definitely quieter. Whether this was totally for Lizzie's benefit, however, Anna wasn't sure.

'About that jewel you've got tucked in your bodice, the one your mother left you.'

Anna's green eyes looked anxiously around the dim cellar of a room. This was a dangerous subject! Several of the women were quite capable of attacking her to gain possession of something as valuable as the heart-shaped pendant which had been bequeathed to her by her French mother.

' 'Tis all right, Anna, I'm speaking low, and most of them doxies are still asleep anyway. No, I was thinking that you could use the jewel to bribe Black Will, and get him to contact your mother's family!'

'Oh, Meg, do you think so?' Anna's eyes glinted with excitement.

'Course I do, love!'

Then the light of hope dimmed, and Anna shook her head sadly.

'No, it won't work. You know that the de la Vigne's cut my mother off without a penny when she married father. She tried to contact them

5

numerous times over the years, but her letters were never answered. And then, when she died, I remember father contacting them to tell them.' She shrugged narrow shoulders under her dirty, threadbare gown. 'They didn't answer him, either.'

'That doesn't count for naught! If you've got any sense in that pretty head of yours, then you'll give it a try, otherwise I doubt you'll get out of here alive. Your sort just aren't cut out for this kind of life, and last time I looked at that leg, it was pretty bad.' Meg's grimy face peered at Anna in the semi-darkness.

'You don't want to lose it now, do you?' She grinned, showing blackened teeth. ' 'Cause if you do, 'tis likely you'll be out on the streets begging, and, take my word for it, that's not much of a life. I should know, many's the time I've had to do it!'

'Yes, you're right, Meg,' Anna agreed, wearily, stretching out a thin hand and patting the woman's shoulder. 'After all, I've got nothing to lose, have I, so I'll give it a try. And, my friend, should it work, I'll not forget you, either. If it hadn't been for you, I'd probably be dead already!'

Anna had slept very little since she'd been hauled off to Newgate, and she certainly didn't expect to fall asleep then, yet she must have, for the next thing she remembered was a sharp poke in the ribs, and Meg whispering to her.

'Wake up, dearie! There's a key turning in the lock, which means that Black Will's coming. Now's yer chance, don't miss it!'

Black Will was a huge, hulking brute of a man. At least six foot two tall, he had a big, ungainly head, and a mass of greasy black hair.

'Right then, you poxy wenches, grub's up!' And he deposited a tray containing a large basket of black, weevil-infested bread and a large pitcher of water, with one solitary earthenware mug, which would be passed from woman to woman.

Some of the women were already on their feet, rushing towards the basket.

'Now there'll be no cheating! Form a queue, and I'll hand you a piece each.'

Meg helped Anna to her feet, and she hobbled along after the older woman, wincing when she inadvertently put too much weight on her injured leg.

When she reached Black Will, he actually smiled at her, and handed her a piece of bread, which, although mouldy, didn't actually have any grubs crawling in it . . .

Anna looked up at him, hating the cruel, lascivious looking face before her, yet knowing that she had no alternative but to try to approach him . . .

'Mr Bates, I was wondering if it might be possible for me to have a word with you in private.'

Will Bates looked surprised, then pleased.

'Why, girl, have you taken a fancy to Black Will, then? Stand to one side, I'll have to finish handing out the bread, then I'll attend to you!'

Trembling slightly, Anna did as he'd said.

She looked at the black bread with distaste, but she knew that if she was going to survive she'd have to eat it, she was already weak with hunger.

At length, Will finished handing out the food, and turned to Anna.

'Right, my pretty! What would you be wanting to say to Will in private, eh?'

Anna took a deep breath, colour rushing into her face. How she longed to strike the hulking brute's hand away! Yet she knew that she couldn't, if she wanted him to consider her proposition . . .

'Mr Bates, I have something of value which I will give you if you'll contact relatives of mine.' She kept her voice very low, so that Black Will had to lean forward to hear what she was saying.

When she had spoken, he threw back his ugly head and laugh.

'And I can guess what, too! Well, well! You are a bold doxy, and you one of the aristocracy, too!' He put his head on one side, considering her. 'Hmm . . . You put a high value on yourself, but I may just consider it!'

'No, Mr Bates, you misunderstand me!' She cried, desperately, catching hold of his sleeve to stop him moving away. 'What I'm offering you is of monetary value, nothing more!'

Will stopped in his tracks, raising one bushy eyebrow.

'Indeed, girl! Well, why didn't you say so before! Right then, just let me retrieve these.' And he picked up the empty tray, mug, and water jug. 'And then you can come with me to my office where we'll discuss this little matter further!'

Black Will's 'office' was a small, dirty room with a desk and a couple of uncomfortable-looking chairs.

There was a half-empty bottle of port, and a bottle of brandy sitting on the desk.

Black Will motioned to Anna to sit down, and then sat behind the desk, lifted the port and brought the bottle to his lips, swallowing noisily.

Then he wiped his mouth with his hand, and waved the bottle towards Anna.

'Drink?'

'No, not port, thank you. But I'd be very grateful for a glass of water.'

Black Will laughed, and slapped his knee.

'I don't keep no water in here, girl! You'll take port and like it!'

Gingerly, Anna took the bottle, wiped the neck, and sipped a little of it.

'It's very good, Mr Bates.' She said, politely, for all the world as if she was having tea in Lady Weathercombe's drawing room. 'But to business. I have a jewel which my late mother left me. If you will get in touch with my relatives in France, it is yours!'

'I see . . . So you're trying to bribe old Will then?' He leaned back in his chair.

Anna hesitated. She would have to be very, very careful. Although she was sure that the gaoler was quite susceptible to bribery, it might well be a hanging offence should he choose to see it in that light . . .

'No, Mr Bates, rather I will give you my mother's jewel as a gift, but I would be very grateful if you would try to contact her relatives, as I've never met them, and would dearly like to!'

'Aye, my dear, I'm sure you would!' Black Will laughed. 'Right then, show me this jewel, and I'll see what I can do for you . . . '

Anna had been frightened that the covetous Will would steal her jewel without having any intention of contacting the de la Vignes. But, thankfully, he didn't.

'Hmm . . . Pretty valuable piece this, if I'm any judge!' he pronounced, after an examination which had lasted the best part of five minutes. 'Very well, Anna Heatherington, give me the address of these relatives of yours, and I'll see what I can do!'

Heartened, Anna wrote down the address on the scrap of paper which the gaoler provided for her.

'You can read it?' she asked, anxiously, as he squinted at the paper.

'Not very well, but I have a learned friend who will be able to, and will write the letter for me, so you've naught to worry your pretty head about there!' He leered at her. 'And now, methinks that a kiss would not go amiss for my pains!'

And before Anna had an inkling of what he intended, he grasped hold of her arms, pulling her from the chair, and into his arms.

Anna staggered, she was weak from hunger and tension, and her leg was giving her a great deal of pain.

'Why girl, what's amiss?' He asked, looking down at her with a vestige of concern.

'Noth . . . ' Anna began, but then the room began spinning around her, and she fainted clean away in his arms . . .

When she came to, Anna found that she was lying in a truckle bed in a small, dimly lit room.

For a few moments, her mind was disorientated. Where on earth was she? Certainly, this wasn't the Heatherington town house in Cavendish Square!

Then it all came back to her, her father's death, and her subsequent removal to Newgate, and she groaned.

So she was still in the hateful place. Yet she wasn't in the dank cell with Meg and the other women, that didn't possess a bed of any description.

She pulled the old, grey blanket to one side, and went to swing her legs off the side of the bed, grimacing with pain as her right one struck the stone floor.

Anna looked down at it warily, not sure of what she would see. But it looked the same as usual. Meg's grimy bandage was still in place.

Using the bed as a lever, she got

to her feet, favouring her injured leg, and hobbled over to a cupboard on top of which was a water jug and glass.

She poured herself some water, and drank it gratefully. Apart from a small sip of Black Will's port, she'd had nothing to drink since the previous evening, and her tongue felt thick and dry.

Then she hobbled over to the heavy, wooden door and tried to turn the handle, but, as she had expected, it was locked.

Well, there didn't seem to be much else to do but return to the truckle bed and wait. Anyway, her leg felt a bit more comfortable when it was raised up.

Anna had been lying there for several minutes when she heard a key turn in the lock.

Her heart leapt in alarm. Surely it could only be Black Will!

But it wasn't. As the door opened, she saw to her relief that it was a plainly, yet neatly dressed middle-aged woman.

'Ah, I see that you've regained your senses!' The newcomer observed, without preamble. There was little warmth in her face or voice.

'Yes . . . Could you tell me, please, where I am?' Anna asked tentatively.

The older woman snorted derisively.

'Surely the surroundings aren't so luxurious that you've already forgotten that you're in Newgate Prison!'

'No, of course not!' Anna replied, with some asperity. 'But I've been moved out of the women's common hold. I wondered why.'

The newcomer shook her head in bewilderment.

'And you're complaining about it? La, girl, but your stay in the common hold must have fair addled your wits!'

'I'm not complaining, I'm glad to be out of it! All I want to know is, why?'

'Well, you should know the answer to that one better than me, after all, my

16

instruction was only to come here and look at that leg of yours!' The muddy brown eyes narrowed slyly. 'Usually, though, if a wench is moved to a side room such as this, 'tis because she has been able to bribe her gaoler.'

So that was it! Black Will had had her transferred to this room because she'd given him the jewel! Well, at least some good had come of it . . .

'Right then,' the woman was saying. 'Pull that blanket back, I'd best have a look at that leg of yours.'

She undid the bandage roughly, Anna wincing, as, with a final jerk, it was pulled free of her leg.

She didn't particularly want to look at it, but she knew she should, so she gazed down at it, her breath catching noisily in her throat as her eyes took in the open, infected sores, and severe, dark bruising.

'Hmm . . . The fetters have done this.' The woman shook her head. 'Why they feel they have to tether you, I'll never know, after all, it's highly

17

unlikely that anyone could get out of the common hold! Still, I suppose it's a way for the gaolers to earn some extra money, seeing as you have to pay to have them struck off! How long were you fettered?'

'Just two days, then a friend paid to have them struck off for me.' As she spoke, a wave of guilt swept through Anna. How was poor Meg faring? When she saw Black Will next, she must ask him if something could be done for the kindly soul . . .

'A good friend you had, then, otherwise you'd have likely lost the leg! Hold still, I'm going to wash some of this muck off for you and put a fresh dressing on it.' As she worked, the woman introduced herself as Margaret Barnes.

'Are you often called into Newgate to help out?' Anna enquired, politely.

Margaret Barnes laughed.

'Now and again. Actually, I'm a mid-wife, but I've gained a fair bit of medical knowledge over the years.

Right, I'll be in again tomorrow to look at that leg of yours, Mr Bates' orders.'

'Thank you.'

'Don't thank me, dearie, thank Mr Bates, it's him that's paying me to do it!'

And with that parting remark, she opened the heavy door, and Anna heard the key turning in the lock outside.

The next two weeks felt endless to Anna, because although the conditions of her captivity had improved enormously, she couldn't help but wonder how long it would actually last.

Would the de la Vignes come to her rescue? Or would they just wash their hands of her, as they had her mother . . .

Anna had given her mother's jewel to Black Will, but kept the gold chain which it had been attached to, so, remembering her promise to Meg to try to get the woman out of the common hold, she had offered the chain to the gaoler on the condition that Meg could join her in the small cell which she now occupied, and, when the de la Vignes came to rescue her — she couldn't tell Will that there was an 'if' — she asked that Meg be allowed to go free and join her.

'Well, this here chain is enough to pay for a few week's lodging in the cell.' Black Will agreed, eyeing the piece of jewellery with avaricious eyes. 'But it isn't enough to buy her out of here, neither is your jewel sufficient payment for you, come to that! No, when these fancy relatives of yours come to claim you, they'll have to pay for your release, plus extra for the woman!'

'But surely that is robbery, Mr Bates! The jewel I gave you was a diamond, and must be worth a small fortune, surely that is enough to pay for Meg and I to leave here!'

Black Will's muddy brown eyes narrowed menacingly, and he pointed a stubby, dirty finger at Anna.

'Just remember, my fine young lady, that you're hardly in a position to bargain! Any more lip from you and you'll be finding yourself back in the common hold, jewel or no jewel!'

Anna bit her lip. Unfortunately, what he said was true, she wasn't in a position to bargain, seeing as the gaoler held all the winning cards.

'Very well, Mr Bates, I agree to your terms!'

And so, that very afternoon, Meg had been brought up from the hold to join Anna.

'Bless you, child, I never thought you'd do it!' She had been pathetically grateful.

'Well, I promised you that I'd try, and I like to keep my promises if I can!' Then her small face clouded over. 'But we're not out of here yet, Meg. In fact, if the de la Vignes don't respond soon, I can quite well imagine Black Will taking a delight in tossing us both back into the hold!'

'Aye, you're probably right there!'

the other woman agreed , ruefully. 'Still, it must take a while to send a message off to France, Black Will must know that, after all, 'tis said he was a sea-faring man in his younger days, and did some travelling.'

'Yes, I suppose it'll take a few weeks. What worries me, though, is that they won't bother to come at all, that they just won't be interested!'

'No, I can't see that.' Meg replied, settling down on the truckle bed which had been provided for her. 'Even if they're not really interested in you, they won't want it to be known that a relative of theirs is in Newgate.' The cunning, slightly blood-shot blue eyes were wry. 'It ain't good for their image, do you see?'

Despite her anxiety, Anna couldn't help but laugh. Meg was certainly helping to cheer her up and making the time seem to pass faster.

'But they're in France, Meg! They've got their own infamous prison there, the Bastille! Why should they care about a granddaughter whom they've never even seen!'

It was Meg's turn to look surprised. 'They're your grandparents? As close as that? Well then, dearie, you've not a thing to worry about, for they'll surely rescue one so closely related to them!'

Meg's conviction that the de la Vigne's would come never wavered. Three weeks had now gone by, and there had been no word whatsoever.

Margaret still came in to dress Anna's leg, and declared that it was healing, although slowly. Anna was now able to walk reasonably well without limping, but when she tried to stand for any length of time, she felt very weak, and her leg tended to give way under her.

Of course, that wasn't entirely due to her leg injury. As the days stretched endlessly on, Anna and Meg found that the provisions which Black Will brought them were deteriorating both in quality, and size.

As they had been when they were incarcerated in the common hold, both

Meg and Anna were constantly hungry. So far, they hadn't complained, as they were afraid that if they did, Will would have them sent back down to the hold.

This morning, however, when Will came in carrying a pitcher of brackish water, a tiny piece of mouldy cheese and a minute piece of meat from which crawled a singularly revolting looking maggot, Anna felt compelled to protest.

'You can take that disgusting offal away again, Mr Bates, and bring us some proper food!' She exclaimed, angrily. 'After all, we're not getting charity, we're paying, and paying very well, for what little you bring us to eat!'

The expression on the gaoler's face would have been ludicrous, only for the fact that he had pretty well life or death authority over both of them, and he knew it . . .

Meg crossed herself, and began muttering a prayer, as Black Will, a look of insane fury on his face, advanced towards Anne menacingly.

His great fist was clenched, and he brought it back, clearly intending to punch Anna in the face.

At that moment, however, the heavy door, which Will hadn't bothered to close behind him, opened, and a tall, well-dressed, slender man entered the room, surveying the tableau before him with a quizzical grin.

'I do hope that I'm not interrupting anything?' he asked, his voice languid.

Black Will dropped his hand to his side, and scowled at the stranger.

'And who would you be, coming in here like this?'

'I was shown to this . . . ' He gazed around the room. 'How does one refer to it? Chamber? Hardly, I wouldn't put my servants in such a room! Anyway, I was shown to this . . . place by a person called Margaret Barnes, who assured me that I would find my cousin, Miss Anna Heatherington, here!'

Anna moved out of the corner where

she'd been cowering when it became clear that Black Will meant to strike her.

'I'm Anna,' she said, tentatively. 'And you must be . . . ?'

He looked down at her then, his handsome face mirroring distaste, so that Anna blushed, realising how dirty and dishevelled she must appear to such a distinguished looking gentleman . . .

He gave her a perfunctory bow.

I'm Julien de la Vigne. My father was your grandfather's first cousin. And now, ma chere, let us not waste any more time in this disgusting hovel!' Gingerly, he took hold of Anna's elbow, propelling her towards the door.

'Oh, but one moment, sir!' Anna exclaimed. 'I want my friend Meg to come with me, she's been very kind to me while I've been imprisoned here!'

Julien paused, surveying the older woman disparagingly.

'Very well.' He nodded. 'If that is what you wish, so be it! I imagine she can act as maid to you!'

Meg rushed forward then with an agility that belied her lengthy sojourn in Newgate, and grasping hold of Julien's hand brought it to her lips.

'Thank you, sir, you'll not be sorry!'

Black Will, who had so far watched the scenario being played out before him in stunned silence, suddenly seemed to realise that his prey would soon disappear without him receiving any further reward.

'Now hold on a minute, sir! You can't just go walking out of here with these women, after all, they're prisoners, held here at his Majesty's pleasure!'

Julien threw him a withering look.

'As you saw fit to inform my family of my cousin's plight, I feel quite sure that you've already been amply rewarded!' He turned to Anna. 'What did you give this fellow to persuade him to send a message?'

'A jewel which I inherited from my mother. A diamond.' Anna replied, truthfully.

'Then, Bates, I consider that you have been well and truly paid already! If you don't agree to let my cousin, who has, after all, been wrongfully imprisoned, and this other . . . person go free immediately, then I shall consider it my Christian duty to inform the prison governor that you are accepting bribes.'

Black Will quailed visibly. He was making a very comfortable living out of accepting bribes, and had no wish to see it come to an end.

'Very well, go, and good riddance to the lot of you!'

2

'But how can we just walk out of here? We'll be accosted!' Anna protested, as Julien led her out into the corridor.

He gave a wry laugh.

'Ma chere, you are very naive! Obviously, when I first came to prison, I saw the governor and obtained a signed pardon for you.' His mouth tightened. 'After all, one does not imprison a member of a noble family such as you come from! The governor proved to be a sensible man, and realised this!'

'But what about Meg?'

'Not of sufficient import for them to bother about, I imagine! But don't fret, if needs be, I'm quite prepared to make a small donation to the prison funds so that she can accompany us.'

'Thank you, you're very kind.' Anna murmured, as indeed, he seemed to be. And yet, something in his face

29

warned her that this might not always be so . . .

Julien showed Anna's pardon to the guard on duty at the gate, and he waved them on, not bothering to ask any questions about Meg.

There was a carriage waiting, and Julien handed Anna in, Meg scrambling up unaided behind her.

'I will sit at the front with the driver.' Julien announced, wrinkling his aristocratic nose, and Anna rightly guessed that he considered that they smelt too unsavoury for him to be in close confinement with them.

'He's a very fine gentleman.' Meg observed, with a wink, as a whip cracked and the carriage sprang forward.

'Yes, yes indeed.' Anna agreed, wondering why she couldn't actually bring herself to like her newly-found cousin . . .

Perhaps it was because she didn't feel at ease with him? Well, certainly, she didn't, after all, it would be very difficult to, when every look he gave her showed her that he despised her . . .

Well, at the moment, she supposed she must look a wretched, despicable creature — but then, was it really her fault?

'Are we driving straight down to the coast and then taking a boat to France?' Meg wanted to know.

Anna shrugged her shoulders helplessly.

'Meg, you were with me all the time, so surely you must know as much as I do! My cousin didn't say what we were going to do, but I would imagine that he means to bring us to some establishment in town so that we can clean ourselves up before embarking on the journey overseas.' She smiled ruefully. 'I don't know about you, but I certainly feel that a long soak in warm, perfumed water wouldn't go amiss!'

'Yes, well I suppose you would feel like that, where I come from, we're not used to such niceties. 'Tis a quick sluice under a cold water pump if you're lucky.'

Anna reached out and patted the

other woman's hand.

'Well things are going to change for you now, Meg, you can be my personal maid, and I promise I won't work you too hard.'

'Then I must get used to calling you Mistress Anna instead of dearie, mustn't I?' Meg observed, with her raucous chuckle.

'I suppose you'll have to in public, but in private, you may call me what you will!' Anna smiled.

Several minutes later, the carriage drew up in front of a smart, fashionable-looking town-house.

Julien stepped down and opened the carriage door.

'We've arrived at our temporary destination, the home of my good friend, Dr Patrick St. Clair.' He held out his arm, and Anna put her hand on it lightly, grimacing with pain as she landed rather heavily on her right leg.

'You have a leg injury?' Julien's dark brows drew together questioningly.

'Yes, I'm afraid my skin proved

rather delicate for the fetters which they put on it! Meg paid for them to be removed after two days, and I am told, by doing so, saved my leg.'

'How dare those scoundrels treat a de la Vigne in such a manner!' Julien exclaimed, angrily.

Anna gave him a rueful smile.

'But to them, cousin, I was not a de la Vigne, but the penniless daughter of a man who had died in a duel owing several thousand pounds!'

'Ah yes, your damned rogue of a father!' Julien shook his head. 'How Louise could have been such an idiot as to marry a man like him, I'll never know! But we are wasting time. Come, let us go inside!'

Anna felt her temper quicken. How dare her arrogant cousin dismiss her poor father just like that! And he hadn't bothered to see whether Meg could manage to get out of the carriage unaided, either!

'One moment, sir! I will wait until

my friend is out of the carriage and with us!'

'My dear girl, now that you are no longer in that hell-hole, I suggest that you refrain from referring to that verminous bag of rags as your 'friend!' People in polite society simply do not have friends of that ilk!'

Anna gave him a withering look, taking in the lean, haughty features, the powder blue, satin waistcoat, and tight-fitting pantaloons in a deeper shade of blue. Her cousin was nothing better than a self-opinionated dandy, so shallow that he could only judge a person by their material possessions . . .

'Please do not speak of Meg like that, for I consider her a much better friend than any that I have previously had in polite society!'

Julien spread his hands helplessly.

'All right, I concede that you are probably bitter at the fact that your former friends abandoned you to your fate. But then, Anna, could you really expect anything else? After all, I have even heard it rumoured that your ignoble father was none other than John Heath, the Hounslow highwayman!'

Anna's face paled, and she swayed, and would have fallen, if Meg hadn't suddenly taken hold of her arm. Could what Julien be saying be true? She had sometimes wondered about her father's nocturnal wanderings . . .

'Sir, you have upset my mistress, and she is very weak! If this is a doctor's house, then I beg that we go in and have him take a look at Miss Anna's leg!'

'You're rather presumptuous, woman, but I'm man enough to concede that you have a point!' Julien swept off his top hat, and gave them a mocking bow. 'Ladies, please proceed!'

The door of Dr St. Clair's house was opened by a severe looking woman with scraped back hair.

Her sour face, however, broke into a smile when she saw Julien.

'Mr Julien! It is good to see you!' Then her nose wrinkled. 'But who on earth are these . . . unfortunates that you have with you?'

'Mrs Rogers, this lady is my cousin Anna, and the other woman will act as her maid. Now, as you can see, these ladies require some attention to their persons, so if we may come inside?'

'Indeed, yes! The doctor is expecting you and the . . . er, ladies?'

'Yes, Dr St. Clair knows all about it!'

'Then if you would be so good as to wait there for a moment, I will tell him that you're here.'

Anna felt faint and weak with fatigue and hunger, yet she forced herself to stand erect, her head held proudly.

A moment or two later, Patrick St. Clair came into the hallway.

He was a tall, handsome man with thick, slightly curling, dark hair.

'Julien, good to see you.' He greeted his friend. Then he turned to Anna and Meg.

'You, I take it, are the unfortunate Miss Anna Heatherington!' And he held out his hand.

'I won't take you hand, as my own is too dirty. Please, sir, do you think I might sit down? My leg is paining me.'

Patrick St. Clair took in the girl's flushed cheeks, which, at the same time, looked almost transparent. She was thin and hunched, all the fire and life gone out of her due to the hardships she had suffered. And yet for all the tattered gown, the dirt and grime, he didn't doubt that she was a beauty . . .

He took hold of Anna's arm, and then, as she swayed a little, scooped her up into his arms as though she weighed no more than a feather.

'Mrs Rogers, take the other woman down to the servants' quarters and organise a bath and a change of clothes for her, will you?' he called over his shoulder, as he strode off with Anna, Julien following behind, an amused smile playing around his mouth.

Patrick St. Clair paused at the foot of

the elaborately carved, oaken staircase.

'Julien, why don't you go into the drawing room and pour yourself a brandy?' The dark eyes twinkled. 'I've some vintage '69 which should appeal to a palate even as jaded as yours! I'll be down to join you after I've taken your cousin up to her room and had a look at this leg of hers!'

'My dear Patrick, how well you understand me!' Julien smiled faintly. 'But if I may make a suggestion? Surely my cousin would feel a great deal better if you were to order one of your maidservants to give her a bath? After all, you hardly want your house to stink of Newgate prison!'

Patrick St. Clair looked down at Anna's flushed face, her green eyes looked enormous against its thinness, and they were dark with shame.

Silently, he cursed Julien for his lack of sensitivity.

'That can come later!' His voice was brusque. 'At the moment, the poor child is exhausted, and her leg is clearly paining her. No, for now, I will attend to her leg, and then she must sleep. Time enough for a bath later!'

'But sir, I don't want to put you to this trouble, and, as my cousin says, I must smell deplorably.' Anna murmured, close to tears.

'This is my house, and I make the rules! Julien, pray go into the drawing room.' And without waiting for Julien to answer, he strode purposefully up the stairs.

Neither Anna nor the doctor spoke until he had laid her down gently on a large, comfortable looking four-poster bed. It's cleanliness was pristine and Anna felt compelled to make a further protest.

'Dr St. Clair, you are being extremely kind to me, but isn't my cousin right? I am infested with vermin, and will quite ruin your beautiful bed!' Then, to her total embarrassment, Anna burst into a flood of tears.

It was like a dam bursting, all her pent-up feelings of the past few weeks coming to the fore now that she was, at last, being shown kindness.

Patrick St. Clair sat down on the bed beside her, and took her into his arms, cradling her to him and patting her head.

He was startled by the strength of emotion that this pathetic, waif-like creature was awakening in him. He had prided himself on being fairly detached from human suffering — after all, in his profession, he had to be.

True, a lot of his patients came from the privileged classes, but he also did quite a bit of unpaid work amongst the poor, never having forgotten the fact that his mother had been a poor Irish gypsy, lifted from hopeless poverty because his father, an enlightened and extremely wealthy French gentleman, had fallen in love with her . . .

But now both his parents were dead, killed in a disaster at sea, when the ship they were travelling on had floundered and sank off the coast of Cornwall.

'You're desperately tired and weak,'

he murmured to Anna, soothingly. 'Forget about my bed.' His finely chiselled lips quirked at the corners. 'Believe me, I have a fair regiments of servants, it will be no problem whatsoever to clean the bed linen!'

Almost with a sense of reluctance, he removed his arms from Anna, propping her up against the pillows.

'And now, that leg, I must assure myself that it is not too badly infected.' And he carefully unwound the bandage applied by Margaret Barnes.

'I'm so ashamed, sir, I didn't mean to break down like that!' Anna's voice was low and tentative.

'Patrick, my name is Patrick, and I'd be pleased if you'd call me that!'

'Then I shall, and thank you . . . Patrick.'

The name sounded strange on her lips. But nice, somehow. Oh, if only her cousin had been more like this man, who had now undone the bandage, and was probing the flesh around her wound with such a light, gentle touch, that

41

Anna didn't even wince . . .

There was a slight frown between his fine, dark eyebrows, and Anna was momentarily alarmed.

'It's not too serious, is it?' she asked, anxiously. 'I won't have to lose my leg, will I?'

'No, my dear, there is no possibility of that whatsoever, so don't fret! Nevertheless, it must have been extremely nasty, and I was just silently railing against a society so unjust that it can put cruel fetters on a gently reared, young lady such as yourself!' He stood up, and pressed a bell.

'What are you doing now?' Anna asked, nervously.

'Just ringing for a maid. I'll need some warm water to bathe the wound before I put some salve and a fresh dressing on it. When she comes, may I ask her to bring you come tea and sandwiches? I would offer you a proper meal, but after the food you will have been getting over the past weeks, it would be far too strong for your stomach, which, I'm afraid, would almost instantly reject it!

'Besides which, you need sleep . . . desperately! Nevertheless, you may well rest easier if the rumblings in your stomach are appeased a little!'

'That would be most welcome.' Anna replied, huskily, a lump forming in her throat. He was so kind and thoughtful, so different from her cousin Julien . . . How on earth had the two struck up a friendship in the first place, she wondered, when they appeared to have absolutely nothing in common! 'But if you don't mind,' she continued, at length. 'I don't think I'll take tea just yet.' She smiled wryly. 'A glass of fresh, clean water would be wonderful, however!'

His dark, compassionate eyes gazed into hers.

'Was it that bad?'

Anna inclined her head, shuddering.

'It was a living nightmare, and one which I just want to forget about, if that's possible! Still, I suppose one good thing did come out of it — Meg!'

'Meg?' Patrick gave her a questioning look.

'Yes, the lady who came out of Newgate with me.'

'Ah yes, you must forgive me. In my concern for you, I'd quite forgotten that you had a companion with you. She was good to you, this . . . Meg?'

'Very good. In fact, it was Meg who paid for the fetters to be struck from my legs.' Anna smiled self-consciously. 'And yet, I had the jewel, and she knew about it, but she refused to take it in payment, telling me that it was worth far too much, and to bide my time, for it might well buy me out of that loathsome place, or, at the very least, pay for better quarters.'

'Then that good lady probably saved your life, Anna Heatherington, and, for that, I shall personally see to it that she is amply rewarded!' And before Anna had an inkling of what he meant to do, he had lifted one of her distinctly grimy hands to his lips.

Violent colour flared into Anna's face, and she pulled her hand sharply away just at the same moment as there was a tap at the door, and, at Patrick's 'Come in,' a neatly dressed maid-servant entered, bobbing a curtsey.

'You wanted something, sir?' To give the girl credit, she was too well-trained to show anything but momentary surprise at Anna's dishevelled appearance.

'Yes, Dorcas, please. I require a bowl of warm water, and my physician's bag. Also, I want you to tell cook to make an assortment of sandwiches for the young lady, and you might also bring me a glass of cold water on your return.'

Dorcas bobbed another curtsey.

'Very good, sir, I'll see to it right away.'

'Whatever must she think, seeing me here?' Anna asked, her voice mirroring her embarrassment, when the servant had left the room.

'No doubt you'll be a nine-day wonder downstairs, but don't worry, my servants are all discreet. Most of them are in my debt one way or another, so they're completely loyal and trustworthy. Now, try and rest for a few minutes until Dorcas returns.'

And the doctor walked over to the window, deliberately surveying the scene outside, although, in all actuality, he saw none of it, his mind was too full of thoughts of the fragile, waif-like girl lying on the bed.

That Julien would take her to France as soon as he, Patrick, pronounced her fit to travel, was a foregone conclusion. And it worried Patrick for he, too, had been living in the French countryside in the region of Nantes, up until a year ago. Then his English paternal grandmother had died, and he had inherited this house.

In France, he had seen the storm clouds gathering. There were frequent uprisings throughout the country, and the village of St Philbert De Grand Lieu, close to where the de la Vigne chateau stood, was becoming increasingly at the mercy of a lawless band of brigands called Dubois.

This family was too extensive to be numbered, and an insolent, blood-thirsty lot they were, too! Patrick had saved the life of one of the Dubois wives who had been in child bed, so he was safe from attack by them. But, nevertheless, when the London house, which he loved, was left to him, he had deemed it wiser to move there, although he still visited France frequently, staying at the ancient manor, which had been his family home.

For, if he wasn't very much mistaken, France was on the brink of revolution, and he doubted that dull, ineffectual King Louis and his flighty, frivolous queen, Marie Antoinette, would be able to do anything to prevent it.

Of course, Julien, being Julien, laughed at his fears, the de la Vignes were a very old, noble family. Who would are to touch them? Certainly not the scavenging peasants!

Patrick St. Clair was not so sure . . .

Dorcas' return interrupted his troubled thoughts.

'There's your bag, sir, and the water you requested. I've ordered the sandwiches, and I'll bring them up as soon as they're ready.'

'Thank you, Dorcas.' Then, as the maid left the room, he handed Anna the glass of water.

She drank it greedily, savouring its cool, clear freshness, after the horrible, brackish water in Newgate.

Then she subsided into a fit of coughing, for she'd swallowed it too quickly.

Patrick patted her back, secretly horrified by the harsh, jutting planes of her shoulder blades.

'Careful, my dear!' he admonished. 'I know that you're very thirsty, but go easy, or you'll make yourself ill.'

'I'm sorry,' she murmured, huskily. 'I shouldn't have drunk it so fast, but it tasted so good after . . . ' Anna handed him the empty glass.

'I know.' He interrupted her gently,

as he put the glass down and opened his surgical case. 'But you'll soon get used to all life's pleasant things once again, I promise you.'

'Yes, I'm sure I will.' Anna found herself answering, dreamily, as her eyes closed of their own volition, and her poor, starved stomach, temporarily satiated by a single glass of water, she found herself falling asleep . . .

Patrick St Clair didn't wake her. He realised that she was absolutely exhausted, and that sleep was the best medicine, even more important than food at the present time.

He worked gently, but quickly and efficiently, on her injured leg, and then, once it was bandaged, he took a blanket from the ornate chest, and carefully put it over her.

Then, satisfied that her breathing was regular, he left the room to join her cousin Julien, closing the door quietly behind him.

When Anna first woke up, she was totally disorientated, looking around the spacious, ornate room in bewilderment.

It was dark, but not pitch. Patrick hadn't closed the thick, gold velvet curtains, so light filtered in through the window from the street below.

Had a miracle occurred? Was she back home? But no, this room was considerably larger than the one which she had used in Cavendish Square, and, as her eyes became accustomed to the glow, Anna saw that the furnishings were much richer than the ones of her former home. They, although respectable, were fairly aged, at least in the upper chambers, her father preferring to use what little money he had to refurbish the rooms which people actually saw.

Then Anna's eyes alighted on a silver tray, on which was placed a plate containing an assortment of dainty sandwiches, a pitcher of water, and a glass.

Her stomach rumbled ominously, and she realised just how hungry she actually was.

Reaching for a sandwich, she pushed it, in its entirety, into her mouth. Then she remembered Dr St Clair's warning, and smiled ruefully.

Forcing herself to eat slowly, Anna managed to consume them all.

Then she drank some water, being careful to take small sips and not huge mouthfuls, as she felt like doing.

Then she settled back down onto the bed, revelling in its exquisite softness.

The next moment, her eyelids had closed again, and she'd fallen into a deep, dreamless sleep.

Anna was awoken the following morning by Dorcas. This time, the maidservant did nothing to hide her curiosity, as she shook Anna into wakefulness.

'Time for your bath, Mistress Anna! Let me help you up, and then I'll help you to disrobe and we can go into the dressing room, adjoining here, where the tub is all ready and waiting for you!

'Lord, mistress, is it really true what

they're saying below stairs, that you're just newly released from Newgate?' her blue eyes were as round as saucers, and Anna, now fully awake, couldn't help but smile.

'Yes, I'm afraid so!' She murmured, letting Dorcas help her out of bed. 'But don't worry, I'm no cut-throat, I was wrongfully imprisoned!'

'I'm sure you were, Mistress Anna. Nevertheless, you're quite a sight, aren't you?' Then she put her hand to her mouth. 'Oh, I'm sorry! I didn't mean to be rude, and if it comes to that, who am I to talk? I was brought up in Gin Lane, so I know full well what it's like to feel the fleas biting!

'Right then, now that we've got that old rag off you, you can slip this robe on and come through into the other room. You'll feel just wonderful once you've had a bath and your hair is washed.'

Anna allowed Dorcas to lead her into the adjoining room, were a steaming tub awaited her, but then she dismissed the maid.

'I can manage very well now, thank you, Dorcas. After all, you've thought of everything.' And she looked around at the soap, towels, perfume and shampoo, in something akin to wonder.

'Aye, well I'll go and strip your bed while you bathe if you like, but then I'll come back and see to your hair for you. I've had some training in hairdressing, and yours, I'm sorry to say, is a right mess! If you want to keep it long, you'd best be letting me do it, otherwise it might need to be cut right off to keep the lice at bay!'

Anna gulped. She had no wish to lose her almost waist-length honey-coloured tresses. She had suffered quite enough humiliation as it was.

'You're right, Dorcas. I'll call you when I've finished bathing and then you can help me with my hair.' She smiled ruefully. 'I must admit, I'm rather fond of it, or, at least, I once was . . . '

'And will be again, Mistress, if I'm not mistaken! You've got a beautiful head of hair beneath all that filth! Right then, let me just test the bath water, and then I'll leave you be. Take as long as you like, Mistress Anna, and then shout to me when you want me to return.' So saying, she went into the adjoining bedchamber, closing the door firmly behind her.

Anna quickly divested herself of her robe and shift, and then climbed into the bath.

She scrubbed herself thoroughly with the expensive, fragrant soap which had been thoughtfully provided for her, and when, at last, she was satisfied that she was scrupulously clean, she got out of the bath and dried herself on the large towel, before wrapping it around herself.

What was she going to wear? she wondered. Perhaps Dorcas would have a suggestion.

Moving over to the connecting doors, she opened them, and called to Dorcas.

'Coming, Mistress!' And the next moment, Dorcas was in the room beside her, picking up the robe and shaking it.

'You can slip this on, Mistress Anna, and then I'll see to your hair.'

'Are you sure that it's clean?' She looked at the garment doubtfully. 'Or have I left a louse or two attached to it?'

Dorcas produced a puffer bottle and squirted some liquid onto the inside of the robe.

'Disinfectant,' she explained, with a cheery smile. 'That'll soon kill off any of the little blighters should they still be foolish enough to hide in there!'

Anna smiled as she put on the robe, and then went over to the built-in, sunken wash basin so that Dorcas could wash her hair.

The shampoo was strong, its fragrance more medicinal than attractive.

'Sorry it smells so foul!' Dorcas

apologised. 'Dr St Clair's orders. It contains various herbs to kill off the lice.'

When Dorcas had finally finished washing Anna's hair, she dried it, partly by the fire which had been made up in Anna's bedroom, and partly with towels.

It was a long and tedious task, particularly as Dorcas insisted on coaxing Anna's hair into an elaborate profusion of ringlets when it was finally dry. Then she handed Anna a mirror.

'Why, Dorcas, that looks wonderful! But where on earth did you learn such arts?'

'Dr St Clair paid for me to receive training in hairdressing.' Dorcas had the grace to look momentarily abashed. 'You see, three years ago now, he caught me picking his pocket. But being the fine gentleman that he is, he didn't hand me over to the law, no, he asked me why I'd tried to rob him, and then, when I told him, he asked me if I'd like to learn an honest trade.

'Well, of course, I jumped at the opportunity, so he had me learn hairdressing and then I came to the house here and was Ladies maid to Mistress Mary-Catherine. But then she died five, six months back, so I've been more or less at a loose end since then.' Her pleasant face brightened. 'That is, of course, until you came along, Mistress Anna!'

'I'm only passing through,' Anna replied, with a wistful little smile. She had a suspicion that she'd be a lot happier if she could remain in this house, presided over by the kind, thoughtful, attractive doctor . . .

'But tell me, who was Mary Catherine?' Images of the doctor's attractive wife floated before Anna's eyes, and, to her shame, she felt jealous . . .

'Mary Catherine was Dr St Clair's mother.' Dorcas smirked. 'And a rum one she was, too! Despite her marrying into the gentry, she was an Irish gypsy, you see, she never really learned how to be a proper lady, never really wanted to, come to that!'

'Oh.' Anna felt a curious sense of relief. So Patrick St Clair didn't have a wife. Well, at least not as far as she knew . . .

'Now, we'd better be getting you dressed.'

'But what in? I haven't got any clothes apart from the ones I wore in Newgate!'

'Don't worry, the doctor said you were to have some clothes of Mistress Mary Catherine's. They're still here in the house, so I took the liberty of selecting some things for you. I'll just fetch them from the next room, and then you can see what you think.'

And before Anna had a chance to reply, Dorcas had hurried off, only to return a few moments later carrying an armful of clothes.

'The gown is mulberry satin, I thought it would set your complexion off nicely.'

'Oh, Dorcas!' Anna breathed. 'It's

beautiful! But are you sure that Dr St Clair won't be annoyed? After all, it did belong to his mother . . . '

'Of course he won't be annoyed! After all, it was he who suggested that you should wear her clothes in the first place!' She grinned impishly. 'When all's said and done, there's not much point in them lying around here gathering dust, now is there? But let's get you dressed, and then you can see what the gentlemen's faces will look like when you appear downstairs in your finery!'

Several minutes later, Anna looked at herself in the floor-length mirror. It seemed as if a different person gazed back at her. Gone was the young, pretty girl of nineteen which she had been when she was living in Cavendish Square, and there was no trace, either, of the dirty, pathetic Newgate waif.

Instead, standing before her, she saw a slenderly beautiful, fashionable young lady. Before, she had still harboured traces of puppy fat, but after Newgate's

59

cruel lesson, there was no more.

Her high cheek bones were clearly defined, her green eyes looked enormous in her small, piquant face.

'Colour,' Dorcas pronounced, interrupting Anna's reverie. 'You need some colour in your cheeks then you'll be perfect! Sit down there by the mirror, Mistress Anna, while I apply some rouge and vermillion for your lips.'

A few moments later, Dorcas stood back, well-satisfied.

'There you are, perfection!'

Anna wouldn't have rated herself so highly, although she had to admit that she looked quite pleasing to the eyes, and certainly very different from the unkempt refugee from Newgate who had come into Patrick St Clair's house the day before . . .

Anna felt curiously nervous as Dorcas led her downstairs to the drawing room, and tapped on the door.

'Come in,' called a languid voice, which Anna recognised as belonging to her cousin, Julien.

With a sense of foreboding, she opened the door, Dorcas having noiselessly retreated in the direction of the servants quarters.

Julien was lounging in a chair, a newspaper in one hand, and a glass in the other. There was no sign of Patrick St Clair.

He looked up as Anna entered, his pale blue eyes darkening as he took stock of her changed appearance.

Then he was on his feet, and moving towards her.

'Anna?' he asked, uncertainly. 'Good god, but I wouldn't have believed it! Cherie, you're a beauty!'

As he spoke, he draped an arm possessively around Anna's shoulders, ushering her to a seat.

Anna felt an instinctive withdrawal from his touch. She found her cousin strangely repellent, and yet she knew, if she was wise, she'd be careful not to show it, at least not too openly . . .

3

'What can I fetch you to drink?' Julien asked, as he moved towards the ornate Mahogany cabinet, took out a bottle of brandy, and poured himself a sizeable measure of the rich, golden-brown liquid.

'Nothing, thank you,' Anna demurred, with a polite smile. 'I've already breakfasted.'

Julien paused, surveying her with a look which was faintly contemptuous.

'My dear girl, your naivety is possibly provincial! I'm not referring to hot chocolate or coffee, I'm asking you to take an alcoholic beverage with me!'

Colour flared in Anna's pale cheeks, and despite her previous resolution not to do anything to anger her cousin, she was stung into retorting.

'Do you then have some impediment with your hearing, sir, that prevents you from comprehending? When I say that I do not require anything to drink, that is what I mean!'

Julien tossed back the brandy, his grey eyes narrowing ominously.

'Tetchy little thing, aren't you? Still, I suppose I can hardly expect you to have learned manners in a place such as Newgate prison!' Then his mood seemed to change, and he laughed. 'Still, it's as well that you show some spirit, otherwise your dear Grandmere Celestine would trample all over you, and no doubt marry you to that pompous prig Antoine de Mandeville!'

Anna leaned forward in her chair, her green eyes anxious. She had absolutely no wish to be married off to anyone! And then, unbidden, a picture of Patrick St Clair flitted into her mind, and she closed her eyes, forcing it to go away.

When she opened them again, her cousin had poured himself another brandy, and was walking towards her, a mocking smile on his lips.

'Well, don't you even want to know any information about de Mandeville, your possible suitor?'

'Whether I do or not, I've a distinct feeling that you're going to tell me!'

Julien shook his head.

'No, not if you really have no wish to know.' And, to Anna's irritation, he picked up a newspaper that was folded on the occasional table next to him, and began to browse through it.

'All right.' Anna sighed heavily. 'If you will be good enough to put aside that newspaper and tell me something of my grandparents and this de Mandeville fellow, I would be most grateful.'

'Good! I thought that your curiosity would get the better of you! Your grandparents are an interesting couple.' He shrugged. 'Well, at least Celestine is, although, her tastes leave something to be desired.' He threw back his haughty, aristocratic head, and laughed.

'You see, little Anna, the fiery

Celestine is not impressed with her husband's cousin. In fact, I'd wager that she sees me as nothing but a wastrel and a ne'er-do-well! And yet, you can see what a fair sort of fellow I really am, for while she considers me thus, I actually admire the woman for her strong spirit.

'Nevertheless, I do not like her! Pierre, now, is a different kettle of fish altogether. He is a small, seemingly insignificant man, and yet he is possessed of considerable shrewdness, and appreciates his cousin Julien's worthiness!' His face took on a pensive quality.

'Forgive me, my dear, but I have been most remiss, and have forgotten to ask you how that leg of yours is. Coming to, I trust? Responding to our good friend Patrick's ministrations?'

During Julien's rambling speech, Anna had realised that her cousin was more drunk that he had at first appeared. She sensed that he was a man of latent violence, and knew that she would have to be careful in her handling of him.

'My leg is feeling considerably better this morning, thank you. And where is the good Dr St Clair?'

'Why, are you missing him already?' Julien replied.

'Of course not!' she stammered, quickly. 'I just wondered where he was, that's all! You must admit, he has been very kind to take me in, and see to my leg, I would like to have the opportunity of thanking him.'

At that moment, the drawing room door, which had been slightly ajar, opened fully, and Patrick St Clair strode into the room, an attractive figure in a dark blue top coat, which swirled around him like a cloak. Carelessly, he tossed the coat to one side, and smiled at Anna.

'Good morning, my dear! I couldn't help but overhear that last remark, I'm afraid, and I assure you, Anna, that there is no need at all to thank me, it's a great pleasure having you here, and I'm only sorry that I wasn't able to greet you when you first came downstairs.' He drew off his gloves, and put them down.

'I was called out on an emergency, but at least it went well. Cissie Chapman and her child will both live.'

Julien raised his eyes heavenwards.

'And that's supposed to be a blessing? My dear Patrick, I don't know why you bother to take on these charity cases. Surely there's enough paupers in the world without you saving their lives and thus swelling their numbers!'

'Cousin Julien, surely you don't mean that?' Anna looked aghast.

'Oh, ignore him, my dear, it is just Julien's way!' Yet Patrick's gaze was sober, as it rested on his friend.

Julien, he knew full well, meant exactly what he said. To a man like him, the lower classes were of less worth than animals, which, for the most part, were at least productive.

It was men like Julien de la Vigne

who were the cause of the current unrest in France. They would bring that fair country to revolution, Patrick was sure of it. And Anna Heatherington would be drawn into the whole sorry mess . . .

Patrick had to admit that Anna's leg had healed well, better, in fact, than he had dared to hope. For that he was glad. And yet, because it had healed so well, Julien was becoming increasingly anxious to return to France, and take Anna away from him.

'Damn it, Patrick I'm not staying here a day longer!' Julien had expostulated, after he, Anna and Meg had been at Patrick's house for six days. 'My cousin Pierre has a coachman waiting to meet us in Calais, at the 'Coq d'Or' and it is madness having him there, living in luxury, costing my poor cousin countless livres when there is absolutely no reason for it.

'You've said yourself that the girl's leg is almost better, Anna is perfectly capable of undertaking the voyage, so what is the problem? Why do you want us to stay on here, eh?' At this point, Julien's face had become calculating.

'Ah! As if I need to ask! You're infatuated with my little cousin, aren't you? Well, hard luck, dear friend! If Antoine de Mandeville doesn't get her, which Celestine will do her utmost to achieve, then little Pierre will get his way and I will marry the girl! But either way, Patrick, cher ami, you will be the loser!'

Patrick's dark face tightened. Sometimes he wondered why he'd bothered to save Julien de la Vigne from drowning in the Loire all those years ago . . .

Certainly, Julien was no asset to mankind in general. He was a selfish, thoughtless aristocrat who thought that everyone else had been put into the world with the sole purpose of doing his bidding! For all that, Patrick knew that he could never have left the other man to drown.

He could still remember the desperate

look on Julien's face as the branch he was holding on to suddenly snapped, and he was carried on the current downstream, his head bobbing up and down, gradually being sucked under the muddy waters of the Loire and eternal oblivion . . .

'There are several words which could easily be applied to you, Julien, but I will not use them! Very well, if you are determined to take that poor girl to France, a country which even you must see is heading towards total anarchy, then I will come with you!'

They left the next day. Anna, Julien, Patrick, and, of course, Meg, Anna's faithful friend from Newgate.

Anna found it difficult to come to terms with the change in Meg, as, indeed, the middle-aged woman found it hard to realise that this lovely, self-assured young lady, was the pathetic waif whom she had tried her best to shield from the worst rigours of Newgate.

Meg was really quite attractive. Forty

one years old, her hair, now that it was clean, was a lovely shade of copper brown.

'This is certainly good fun!' She chuckled, looking out across the vast expanse of sea, as she and Anna stood on the deck of the Queen Charlotte, the vessel which was taking them to France, and a new life . . .

'We're fortunate to have such a good crossing, I think!' Anna smiled back at her. 'I've never been on a ship before, and didn't really know what to expect! But this, as you say, is good fun!'

'It's nice to see you looking so well, milady,' Meg observed, looking at the young woman whom she thought of as her charge quite fondly.

'There's no need to call me 'milady' ' Anna replied. 'As we agreed before, when we're alone, you must call me Anna!'

'No, I don't think so. You belong in a different world to someone of the likes of me! Still, I can call you 'Miss Anna' if that would please you better?'

'Call me what you will.' Anna replied, and meant it. Yet she felt a slight feeling of sadness, as she realised that Meg was right. From now on, they did belong in different worlds, and, in those weeks in Newgate, Meg had been the only friend whom Anna had possessed. Of course, Patrick St Clair was with them, and he seemed very kind. But he was disturbingly attractive, and Anna knew that she should try to keep out of his way.

The de la Vignes obviously had their own ideas of whom they wanted her to marry, and although she intended to fight tooth and nail against any arranged match which was unpleasing to her, she was sensible enough to realise that they would be her guardians, and her benefactors.

Without the de la Vignes, she would be a penniless felon in Newgate. So she supposed that she owed them some loyalty, even if it meant sacrificing her own happiness . . .

They arrived in Calais in pouring

rain. Julien, scowling because his fine, new velvet top-coat was getting wet, quickly hailed a cab, and they headed off in the direction of the 'Coq d'Or.'

They were shown into a private parlour, where they were served with drinks while they waited for their meal.

Patrick had overruled Julien's objections to having Meg dine with them.

'This lady has done us an admirable service in looking after Anna to the best of her abilities while they were both in that most unhappy of places. The least we can do is to see that she is served the same excellent repast as ourselves.'

Julien scowled, and maintained an aloof silence throughout the meal, which was, indeed, quite excellent. There was a thick, nourishing stew crammed full of rabbit meat and seasonal vegetables, followed by a most succulent pigeon pie, served with potatoes and vegetables marinated in red wine sauce, and then a tempting array of sweetmeats.

Anna, realising that the fare was very rich, ate sparingly, knowing that her stomach was still not used to such delicacies.

Meg, however, was not so prudent, and she had scarcely finished her meal when she suddenly rushed from the table clutching her stomach.

'Oh, Lawk's a Mercy, but I'm going to be ill!' she exclaimed, pitifully.

Patrick was immediately on his feet, and handing her his kerchief, ushered her from the room before too much damage was done.

Julien's lips curled contemptuously.

'What a fool Patrick is sometimes! Fancy inviting a woman of that calibre to dine with us! Well, it'll serve him right if she's sick all over him!'

Anna didn't actually trust herself to reply, instead, she got to her feet, and headed for the door.

'Where are you going?' Julien, for all his apparent languidness, could move quickly if he chose to, and now he was behind her, his long, slim, pale hand resting lightly on the shoulder of her blue, soft, woollen travelling dress.

'To see if Meg's all right, of course!'

'You forget, dear cousin, that your jailbird friend is in good company! After all, Patrick is a doctor, and must surely be better qualified to help the creature than you can be! Please, sit down and finish your meal,' he said, leading her back to the table. 'Why don't you try one of these strawberry sweetmeats? I do declare, they are quite delicious!'

'I suppose I could have one,' Anna replied, grudgingly.

Julien picked up one of the little sweetmeats, stood up, and moved over to behind Anna's chair.

'Open your mouth!' he commanded, his voice slightly husky.

Anna whirled around, and snatched the sweetmeat from his hand.

'There is no need for you to be quite that helpful, cousin.' Her voice was decidedly cold.

'Really, cherie!' Julien laughed. 'You are quite a prig and a spoilsport. Perhaps you'll make an admirable wife for the dull de Mandeville after all!'

Anna put the sweetmeat down on her plate with the rest of her discarded food. Somehow, it had lost its appeal.

'Who is this de Mandeville fellow whom you keep mentioning?' She demanded, a faint tremble in her voice betraying her anxiety just as much as any words could.

'He was your mother's suitor. He was totally heartbroken when the fair Louise upped and ran off with your father. He remained a bachelor for several years afterwards, and then it was said that he only married because he needed an heir to carry on the de Mandeville name.

'His wife died in child bed a number of years ago, and no-one has tempted him since.' He gave a wicked smile. 'But then, he hadn't met you, had he? And you are the living image of Louise as she was at that time!'

76

'How can you know that? You cannot possibly remember her!'

'Yes, indeed you are right. But although your grandparents never forgave your mother for her most . . . unfortunate marriage, they never really forgot Louise, you will find portraits of her all around the chateau de la Vigne.

'One, I understand, was completed on the day that her betrothal to Antoine de Mandeville was announced, and that very same night she stole from her room and rode off into the darkness with your father.'

'You make it sound very romantic.'

'Oh, I suppose it must have been, in its way! Yet it was deplorably foolish of Louise. After all, de Mandeville is one of the richest men in the province, and he was comparatively young in those days, too!'

'And now he is old, and no doubt embittered, and my grandmother wishes to marry me off to him! Oh, cousin Julien, what are you leading me into?'

'Come, Anna, things are not as black as they may seem. After all, that is Celestine's wish. Pierre, I think, feels differently.'

'He does?' Anna looked at him with an expression of hope in her eyes.

'Yes, dear cousin. In fact, if I'm not mistaken, I feel sure that your esteemed grandpere would not look unkindly on myself as a possible husband for you!'

'Oh no!' Anna exclaimed, involuntarily. Then she realised that she must be sounding appallingly rude. 'What I mean to say is, no, I don't know you! I would need to know someone before I could happily think of marrying him!'

Julien reached out and stroked the hands which Anna held tightly clasped together. Instinctively, she drew away, and his cold, handsome face hardened.

'I am not a leper, you know, cousin! I may tell you that I have always met with considerable favour from the ladies!'

Fortunately, at that moment, the door burst unceremoniously open, and

Patrick re-appeared, brushing a hand through his slightly rumpled, dark hair.

'All's well, Meg is safely abed!' He exclaimed, quite cheerfully. Then he became aware of the very tangible tension from the couple who were sitting, side by side, but very upright, at the table in front of him.

Patrick's face tightened. What had Julien being doing to upset Anna?

4

They left at dawn the following morning after spending a comfortable night at the inn.

The coach that was to take them to Nantes bore the de la Vigne arms, and was very grand. It had sumptuous gold velvet seats, so deliciously soft, that Anna felt as if she was sinking right down into them.

As he appeared to prefer to do, Julien was once again sitting up on top with the driver, an aged, haughty retainer of the de la Vignes.

Anna wasn't sorry, too much of her cousin in close proximity was becoming increasingly un-nerving to her.

She was, however, quite anxious to know more about the de la Vigne chateau, so she decided to ask Patrick about it.

'Considerably superior to my house,

that's for sure! Yet, for all that, I like to think that my humbler abode has a more lived-in feel about it.' He continued, musingly, and Anna saw that although he was looking at her, he wasn't really seeing her. Clearly his mind was visualising the two dissimilar dwelling places.

'The chateau is very beautiful, of course. It's very large, and has a moat, and it dates back to the early sixteenth century. Apparently, it was a gift to one of your noble ancestors, Henri de la Vigne, for services rendered to King Henri 2nd.

'It's been extensively modernised since then, of course, but it has been so carefully done that you would be unlikely to be able to tell, except for the additional comfort. It also has a great many hectares of land, ornamental gardens complete with fountains and statues of the Muses. In short, the chateau de la Vigne is a miniature paradise. It has everything that could be desired.'

Meg had been listening with her head cocked to one side.

'If it's so bloomin' wonderful, why don't you like it?'

Patrick threw back his head and laughed.

'You're a bright one, Meg, was it so obvious?'

'Aye, so it was, sir, with every word that you said!'

'Yes, I definitely got that impression, too.' Anna nodded gloomily. 'After all, you even said that your house has a more lived-in feel about it, and I can quite believe it! I suppose that's it, really. The chateau's too big, and cold, and am I right in surmising that the people who live in it aren't too friendly either?'

Patrick hesitated momentarily before answering. He wanted to be truthful with Anna, but he didn't want to frighten her off, either.

'No-one could possibly call your grandmother a warm person,' he replied, guardedly. 'But, for all her cold exterior, I'm sure that she means well. After all, these are difficult times that we live in and . . . '

As if to emphasise his words, a small volley of stones suddenly struck the window against which Anna had been leaning. She drew back involuntarily with a little gasp of surprise.

The hatch leading to the front of the carriage was suddenly flung open, and Julien called.

'Damned peasants, they're actually stoning us! Are you all right in there?'

'Perfectly,' Patrick replied, tight-lipped. 'But Julien, don't you think it might be wiser for you to continue the journey inside?'

'No, dear Patrick, I don't! This way, if the scum get too much out of control, I can shoot at them, pick them off like grouse! No, mon ami, I have absolutely no intention of seeking the sanctuary of the coach unless it should rain as it did yesterday. Then, I will certainly join you!' And, without waiting for a reply, he slammed the hatch shut once again.

'I get the feeling that we ain't too popular here,' Meg observed, with a woebegone grin. 'Why's that? Don't they like the Vines?' By that, Anna and Patrick correctly assumed that she meant the de la Vigne family.

It was Patrick who answered.

'Meg, my dear, this country is fast approaching total anarchy.'

Meg looked totally bewildered, and despite her recent fright, Anna couldn't help but laugh at the expression on her face.

'The doctor means that France is becoming more and more lawless.' She interpreted. Then she turned to Patrick. 'Is that true?' Then, without waiting for him to answer. 'Well, I suppose that, judging by those stones that hit the coach, it must be! Was it because of the de la Vigne coat of arms, do you think?'

'Yes, I'm afraid so.' Patrick nodded. 'They're one of the most ancient families of France, and, in these times, that won't stand them in good stead!' He laughed, but the laugh was a mirthless one. 'Sorry, Anna, for a moment I'd quite forgotten that you were one of them! You're not like them, you know.'

'I'm not?' Anna looked surprised. 'But Julien assured me that I was the mirror image of my mother, Louise. For myself, I couldn't say, for she died in childbirth with my little brother when I was but two years old.'

'Ah yes, the portraits of Louise de la Vigne. She was your grandparents' only child, wasn't she? They must have loved her an awful lot, even though they chose a strange way of showing it! In my description of chateau de la Vigne, that was one thing I left out. The place is liberally scattered with portraits of Louise. And yes, Anna, to answer your question, you do look very like her.'

'And yet I don't resemble my grandparents?'

'You have a faint look of Celestine, she must have been quite a beauty in her day. Pierre, no. He is, physically, quite an insignificant-looking man, yet I suspect that he may well possess more character than we give him credit for.'

'They sound a right miserable pair!' Meg observed, with a scowl. 'Lord, Anna, I mean Miss Anna, I'm starting to wonder if we wouldn't be better off in that cess-pit we was in, than coming to this God-forsaken place where they don't seem to want us!'

'It's not levelled at you personally, Meg.' Patrick smiled. 'In fact, I think that most of the populace would be in favour of you. It's people like the de la Vignes they don't like. The aristos.'

'Aristos? You mean like the nobility?'

'Exactly.'

Anna's eyes widened, making her face look smaller than usual, the high cheekbones clearly defined.

'But if that's the case, Patrick, doesn't it mean that France is on the brink of a revolution?'

Anna felt curiously bereft after they dropped Patrick off at his home. She couldn't see it very well, due to the darkness, but to her, it seemed very substantial, and as the chateau de la Vigne seemed to be considerably larger, she knew very well that she was going to feel lost indeed!

Patrick had promised to call on them soon, which should have helped, but, strangely, didn't, and Anna was forced to admit that she was suffering from an attack of nerves at the prospect of meeting her unknown grandparents who had so callously abandoned her mother . . .

Anna looked out through the window. The blackness was infernal, so she couldn't actually see anything, and yet she seemed to sense a wild desolation, occasionally making out the outline of a skeletal tree, made ghostly, and threatening, by the darkness.

'Cheer up, Miss Anna,' Meg was saying. 'It's been a very long day, and, like as not, you're feeling very tired. As me old Ma used to say, when you feel tired, the brain plays tricks and . . . '

At that moment, several shots rang out, shattering the dank night air like cannon fire.

The window of the coach was hit, shards of glass flying around the interior like seaweed spewed up by a ruthless winter sea.

'What . . . what was that?' Anna whispered, fearfully.

But Meg was in no condition to answer her. The bullet which had hit the coach window had lodged in her temple, and she was slumped down on the coach seat.

'Oh Lord!' Anna cried, aloud, and at the same time as she took in her friend's condition, the coach veered madly to right and left, the horses clearly out of control, before coming to rest in a ditch.

Anna was thrown off her seat onto the floor of the carriage, striking her head, so that for a few moments she was totally disorientated, and didn't realise where she was.

Then the coach door was wrested

open, and Julien was standing there, his face ghostly in the pale moonlight.

'Are you hurt?' he barked at her.

She shook her head, wincing slightly at the pain which coursed through it as she did so.

'No . . . no, I'm all right. But Meg is hurt, look, there is blood on her forehead! Oh, Julien, she's not dead is she?'

'Our driver is injured.' He leapt into the coach, and pulled Meg unceremoniously out.

'Please, Julien, be careful with her!' Anna entreated, following them out onto the muddy country lane.

'Don't fret, she'll live!' Julien remarked, grimly, as he laid Meg down on some grass at the side of the lane, alongside the wounded coachman, who was groaning and fingering a wound to his chest from which blood was seeping.

'Who would do such a thing?' Anna asked, her voice unsteady. 'Was it footpads? But no, it cannot have been, for they haven't stolen anything!'

'It was the Dubois.' Julien replied, his face set in harsh lines.

'The Dubois?' Anna queried. 'But who are they, and why should they want to attack us?'

'They're peasant scum, and I intend to hound the bloodthirsty devils into the ground! Right, Anna, you stay here, while I take one of the horses and seek them out. I don't think the attack was perpetuated by many of them, one, maybe two. But, as I live, I swear that I'll get even with them!'

'But what about Meg and the coachman? They may die unless they get medical attention! Would it not be wiser to forget these people, the Dubois, and ride over to Patrick's house and tell him what has happened?'

'Later! They can wait until later! At the moment, there is more pressing business to attend to!' And he leapt up onto one of the horses backs and rode off into the darkness without a backward glance.

Anna sank down onto the grass, her legs suddenly feeling weak and useless. She stuffed one hand into her mouth to prevent the tears which threatened to come from actually falling.

What on earth was she to do? She was no nurse, and she was out here all alone with two injured people. Let alone the threat of the bloodthirsty Dubois, who might return at any moment and subject her to heaven knows what!

Then Meg gave a faint whimper, and Anna's equilibrium reasserted itself.

'Meg, can you hear me?' She cradled the woman's head in her arms.

'Yes, dearie, but what's happened? Me head feels like it's on fire!'

'You've been injured, Meg, our coach was attacked by some ruffians. But just you lie still, everything will be all right, I promise you. Julien's gone off in search of help.'

Anna hoped that God would forgive her for the lie, but it seemed to soothe Meg, and so she turned her attention to the coachman.

His wound was still oozing blood quite badly, so she tore off a strip from her petticoats, and bound it around his chest as best she could.

Fortunately, he was a small, light man, so she didn't have too much trouble in lifting him.

Nevertheless, she was quite tired from her efforts, and shaking with cold, and delayed shock, when she suddenly heard the thundering of horses hooves coming towards her . . .

Oh God! It must be one of the Dubois, coming to kill her! What on earth should she do? Try to hide? But that would mean abandoning Meg and the coachman to their fate . . . Would she be able to reason with the fellow? Perhaps try and bribe him? Her mind was a mass of chaotic, frightened thoughts.

And then it was too late, the horseman was there, in front of her, leaping down from his horse, and she saw, to her profound relief, that it was Patrick.

'Anna, are you all right?' he asked, raggedly, striding towards her and pulling her into the warm, comforting circle of his arms. 'What on earth happened?'

'Oh Patrick! Thank goodness you're here! We were fired upon by some ruffians, Julien said they would be the Dubois, and Meg and the coachman have been injured! I think I've managed to stem the flow of blood from the coachman's chest wound, but I haven't been able to do anything for poor Meg, and she has a head wound!'

Gently, Patrick released Anna, and went over to the injured pair lying on the grass verge, where he quickly, but deftly, examined them.

'Don't worry about your friend Meg,' he said, after a few moments. 'It's only a flesh wound. The bullet has grazed her forehead and stunned her, but no real damage has been done. The coachman's injury is worse, but, as you say, you've managed to prevent further blood loss, and that's really all that can be done until we get him back to the chateau.' For the first time, he seemed to become aware of the fact that Julien was missing. 'But where's Julien? Has he ridden back to the chateau to seek help?'

'No, he insisted on going after the Dubois.' Anna bit her lip.

'The selfish, arrogant fool! Do you mean to tell me that he left you here all alone just to satisfy his own lust for vengeance?'

'I tried to remonstrate with him, but he wouldn't listen.'

'No, a man of Julien's calibre wouldn't, which is why this country is in the mess it is today!'

'But what made you decide to come after us? Had you forgotten something?'

'No.' Patrick shook his head. 'But I am aware of the de la Vigne's unpopularity in this area, and I was afraid that such a thing might happen! Thank goodness that I had the sense to obey my instincts!'

'I'm very glad that you did,' Anna replied. 'I must confess that I was starting to feel quite nervous being out here, and then, when I heard your horse approaching, I thought that you must be one of the Dubois, and I . . .'

But Patrick had pulled her into his arms, and cupping her face with one of his strong hands, was looking into her eyes with great warmth.

'My poor darling,' he murmured, as he bent his head so that it was only inches away from her lips. 'I'm so sorry! The last thing in the world which I would willingly do is frighten you, surely you know that?'

Anna knew that he was going to kiss her. She should pull away, and yet, somehow, she couldn't, she felt as if she was rooted to the spot . . .

A mocking laugh suddenly tinkled on the air, and Anna and Patrick drew guiltily apart just as Julien dismounted from his horse.

'What a touching little scene! Pray,

do not stop on my account!'

Colour flared into Anna's cheeks — she felt horribly embarrassed. Patrick, however, was furious.

'What the devil do you think you're playing at, Julien, going off and leaving Anna alone with two injured servants when you know perfectly well that this area is infested with Dubois hungry for your blood!'

'Well, at least there will be one less to hunger after it now!' Julien retorted, with a mocking grin. 'I managed to kill the fellow who was responsible for this night's work! Little more than a child, he was. Sixteen at the most, I'd say, but that monstrous clan grows up quickly!'

Anna shuddered. All right, so the Dubois shouldn't have fired at the coach, but even so, there was something rather obscene about the way in which Julien was standing there gloating about killing someone who was so young . . .

'Perhaps that 'monstrous clan' have

had to grow up quickly.' Patrick rejoined, soberly. 'After all, they have scarcely had an easy life, France has known hardships and famine these past few years.'

'My dear Patrick, you sound as if you care about the worthless scum!'

'Julien, often I find myself wondering why I ever bothered to pull you out of the Loire! Sometimes I think that I would have been doing mankind in general a greater favour if I'd let you die!'

'Huh! You couldn't have done it!' Julien sneered. 'And you know why, Patrick St Clair? Because you're soft, it's the bourgeoisie blood in you!'

Anna had been listening to the exchange in silence, now she felt that it was time she intervened.

'Gentlemen, may I remind you both that while you stand here arguing, there are injured people here! If you wish to quarrel, that is up to you, but surely you can get these people back to the chateau first!'

'I'm sorry, Anna.' As he spoke, Patrick picked up Meg and set her on his horse, climbing up behind her. She was conscious once again now, but a little disorientated, wanting to know where she was, and why she was going out riding in the middle of the night.

Patrick explained to her what had happened, and then turned back to Julien.

'You can take the coachman back on your horse, Julien. But be careful, his wound is quite deep, you will need to travel slowly if it is not to re-open.'

For once, Julien made no argument, but did as he was bidden.

'I assume you are able to ride?' Patrick asked, turning to Anna.

'Yes, I often rode with my father.' As she spoke, images of her father formed in Anna's mind, and her eyes filled with tears. Oh, what was the matter with her? Surely now, of all times, she wasn't going to cry! She blinked a couple of times, forcing them away. But not before Patrick had noticed.

'Don't worry, Anna, dear, things will be all right.' His voice was low and tender, meant for her ears alone, although it was probable that Julien, at least, heard it.

If he did, however, he made no comment, and Anna climbed up onto one of the two remaining horses.

'What about the other one?'

'We'll send a groom back for it.' Julien replied. 'Now, cousin, let us recommence our journey, your grandparents will be wondering what on earth has happened to detain you!

They arrived at the chateau in the early hours of the morning, where, despite the lateness of the hour, Celestine de la Vigne was waiting in the Sevres drawing room to receive her granddaughter.

Julien accompanied Anna, Patrick having gone to attend to the coachman and Meg's wounds.

Anna's heart felt as if it was fluttering like a butterfly, as a servant announced her, and a voice from within, cold, clear, and autocratic, bade her enter.

Julien gave Anna a push forward, and, for once, she was grateful to him, as she felt as if her legs had become leaden, and would no longer carry her along.

Then she was in the room, Julien behind her, sweeping a courtly bow to the woman enthroned on an antique chaise longue.

Anna regained her wits sufficiently to drop a graceful curtsey, and then the majestic figure before her stretched out a slender arm, and beckoned her to come forward.

'Julien, you may go!' the voice said, haughtily. 'As even you should be able to imagine, I wish to speak with my granddaughter alone!'

Anna didn't dare turn round to steal a glance at Julien's face, but she did have to stifle a slightly hysterical desire to giggle. The thought of Julien being dismissed just like a naughty schoolboy was quite amusing.

Then she had no further time for

thought, as she was directly in front of her grandmother, gazing into a face that must once have been beautiful.

Celestine was thin to the point of emaciation, even her elaborate, gold and black satin gown couldn't disguise the fact. Her hair was ornately styled and powdered, but the face below was wrinkled, the mouth curved downwards, as if its owner had known much suffering.

'Louise!' Celestine's breath seemed to come in painful, rasping gasps.

'Grandmother, are you all right? Shall I go and fetch some help?'

Celestine shook her head, and gave Anna the travesty of a smile.

'Forgive me,' she murmured, at length. 'It was the shock, you see. You are very like my little Louise, and for a moment, well, I forgot that time had passed and I thought that you were her! I hope that I did not frighten you?'

'Well you did a little, Madame,' Anna replied, truthfully.

'No, not Madame. I would prefer it if you would call me grandmother, or, when we are speaking in French . . . you do know your mother's language?

'Yes, although I have not had a great deal of occasion to practise it.'

'No matter, I will see that you become fluent! Yes, when we speak together in French, which we shall, then you will address me as grandmere.'

'I understand, Grandmother!'

'Good, then sit down, dear Anna, and tell me about your journey here. You are very late, I trust that you did not meet with a mishap?'

Anna was surprised. She'd assumed that her grandmother would have been informed right away of the attack on the de la Vigne carriage. But perhaps there hadn't been time. Certainly, she hadn't been given a moment to tidy up before having been ushered into the old lady's presence.

Quickly, she explained why they had been delayed, and two stark patches of colour appeared on Celestine de la Vigne's pale cheeks.

'How dare that riff-raff attack the coach bringing my granddaughter back home to me!' she cried, in a voice which trembled with rage. 'I swear that I will personally go to the authorities tomorrow and make those fools who are supposed to be keeping law and order send out men to arrest the whole family of Dubois and clamp them in irons where they belong!'

'Oh no, Grandmother, I don't wish to cause any trouble, and, besides, Julien gave chase, and killed the Dubois responsible for the attack.'

'Hmm . . . I don't normally see much good in your grandfather's cousin, but in this instance, I see he is to be applauded! Very well, my child, I shall take no further action on this occasion.' She gave a mirthless laugh. 'Anyway, the authorities are becoming increasingly powerless.

'Even if a person such as I was to go after them, I doubt they would have the resources to bring those filthy Dubois to justice!' She shook her head sadly. 'Oh, my dear child! Glad as I am to have you with me at last, I could wish that you were visiting France at a happier time!'

5

Although she was feeling desperately tired, Anna found it very difficult to get off to sleep that night — well morning, really, as it was gone three a.m. when she tumbled into the luxurious four-poster bed which was the central feature of the huge, lavishly furnished room which had been assigned to her.

It was Louise's former room, and Anna doubted very much that anything had been altered since her mother had inhabited it.

There was an ornately framed portrait of Louise over the large, marble fireplace, and Anna had spent several minutes standing in front of it, staring at it.

It was slightly unnerving, in some ways, particularly as she had no recollection at all of Louise, having been scarcely two when she'd died.

Possibly that was one of the reasons why she was so restless. She had the uncanny feeling that she had stepped back in time, at least in Celestine's eyes, and she knew that she would have to struggle to maintain her own identity.

Eventually, she fell asleep, but even then, her dreams were troubled. She woke up bathed in perspiration, although, in reality, the night was a cold one.

After that, she kept the lamp burning, and managed to sleep without further disturbance until a tap at the door awakened her.

Anna sat up in bed and rubbed her eyes. For a moment or two, she was totally disorientated, as she took in the palatial splendour of the room, but then, with a slight sense of unease, she remembered . . .

'Come in,' she called, as the tap sounded again. Then it struck her that her visitor might not speak English, so she shouted 'Entrez, s'il vous plait.'

The door swung open noiselessly,

and a tall, pretty girl entered the room.

'You have slept well, Mademoiselle?' she asked Anna, in French.

Anna had to think for a moment or two to find the right words. Indeed, her French was decidedly out of practice, and she felt sure that her grandmother would be quite displeased with her.

'Not very well, but I think that was because I was over-tired due to the lateness of the hour. The bed itself is most comfortable, and the room beautiful.'

The blonde girl smiled.

'Yes, it is a lovely room, is it not? I understand that it was your mother, Mlle Louise's room, so no doubt the mistress thought that it would be a fitting choice for you. But I am being most remiss, I should be introducing myself to you. I am Charlotte Dupont, and Madame de la Vigne has chosen me to be your personal maid.' She smiled shyly. 'I hope that arrangement will be agreeable to you?'

'I should imagine that if my grandmother has already decided, then it will have to be!' Anna exclaimed, with a wry grin.

She had hoped that Meg would have been her personal maid, but the girl in front of her did look very pleasant. How was Meg faring anyway? She would have to hurry up and get dressed and find out . . .

'I'm sure we'll get along very well.' She smiled at Charlotte. 'We must be of about an age, I would think. I'm nineteen, how old are you?'

'Eighteen, Mademoiselle. Now, what would you like me to do first? Pour your bath, or arrange for breakfast to be brought up to you?'

'Oh, I don't want breakfast in bed!' Anna exclaimed, hastily. 'Actually, if you'll just fetch me a basin and jug of hot water, along with some towels, I'll wash and dress. I'm quite anxious to go and find out how my friend . . . I mean my servant, Meg is after the injury she received last night.'

'There's an adjoining bathroom, Mademoiselle, where I think you'll find everything you need. As to Madame Meg, I thought you would wish to know how she was progressing, so I made enquiries before coming to you. She is resting in bed today, Dr St Clair's orders, but she's conscious and perfectly lucid, and should be capable of being about her duties tomorrow.'

Anna frowned. She was very relieved to know that Meg was doing well, but what did Charlotte mean by 'her duties?' Had Celestine already assigned work for Meg?

'What work is Meg to do?' she asked, at length.

'Cook did tell me that Madame had told her that Meg was to serve as a scullery maid.' Charlotte looked embarrassed.

'A scullery maid!' Anna was outraged. A scullery maid was about the lowest position possible in a noble household, usually reserved for young girls of little more than twelve or thirteen, and there was no way that Anna intended to sit back and let her friend, who had shown her such kindness, be humiliated.

'Neither Cook nor I thought it was right, Mademoiselle Anna, but well, there was nothing we could do about it, Madame's word is law here.'

'We'll see about that!' Anna retorted, grimly. 'Charlotte, find me something to wear, will you? You'll find my wardrobe sadly limited, I've only got some garments which Dr St Clair was good enough to let me have, they belonged to his dead mother. I'll just go and freshen up, and let you know when I'm ready.'

Despite her anger, Anna couldn't help but be impressed by the splendour of the bathroom, which included warm, running water.

She would have liked to have taken a bath, but she wanted to see her grandmother as soon as possible, so she contented herself with a quick, but thorough wash, and then, when she was dry and dressed in her undergarments, she called for Charlotte.

Charlotte had selected one of Catherine St Clair's most elegant gowns, a morning gown in a flattering mulberry velvet.

It suited Anna's fair colouring to perfection and when she was finally ready, she felt composed enough to face her grandmother . . .

Anna eventually found Celestine in her bedchamber, sitting at her escritoire writing a letter.

She looked up as Anna entered, and the latter was disturbed to see that in the cruel light of the April morning, her grandmother looked even more frail than she had appeared the previous night.

'Why, Anna, cherie, this is a pleasure! Do sit down. You have slept well and breakfasted, I trust?'

Anna shook her head.

'I didn't sleep very well, but that was due to being overtired, and the trauma of the day, I think. I haven't yet breakfasted, having heard some news from Charlotte which disturbed me, and having wished to discuss it with you first.'

'Then pray, speak! If there is one thing that I have no patience with, it is ditherers! If something is not to your liking, my child, then I would hear it!'

Her manner was formidable, and despite her resolve, Anna felt a qualm of nerves.

'It's about the lady who accompanied me here,' she began.

'Lady? My dear, you must refresh my memory, for I remember no lady. Two gentlemen, yes, and two injured servants. Who, pray, is this lady?'

Anna's hands were clenching and unclenching on her lap, and she felt hot temper rise inside her. How dare her grandmother bait her like this! Angry words were forming on her lips, but then she took another look at Celestine's transparently pale face, and she forced them back.

'Very well, Grandmere, maybe I didn't word that correctly, and yet I feel sure that you must know what I meant! I was referring to Meg Skeels, with whom I shared a cell in Newgate, and whose kindness most probably saved my life!'

Celestine's face was as hard and cold as if it had been hewn out of granite.

'Granddaughter, don't let me ever hear you say that you were sharing a cell in Newgate with that woman again! That part of your life is past, dead! If you are going to continue to remember, and make reference to it, then I fear it will be necessary to send this . . . person . . . away from you forever!' As she finished speaking, she threw back her head, her eyes raised heavenwards.

'I can see from your face, Anna, that you think me an unpleasant, selfish old woman, and yet I am only thinking of you when I say these things. That woman is part of a past that you have to forget. You are a noblewoman and she is a peasant. There is a world of difference between you. No good can come of harbouring friendships with one such as she!'

Anna looked at her grandmother with an expression that was almost pitying.

'I know you think that you're right, Grandmere, but you're wrong, horribly wrong! And I fear that one day you'll live to regret it! I don't intend to plead with you, so all I'll do is tell you. If you send Meg away from this place, then I shall go with her! If you make her work as a scullery maid, then I will harbour resentment towards you, instead of loving you, which is what I would like to do.

'Perhaps she could serve afternoon teas and the like, or, much as Charlotte seems a pleasant enough sort of girl, I would much prefer it if Meg could serve me as my personal ladies maid.'

'Never!' Celestine de la Vigne spat out the word. 'That Cockney scum will never serve as my only granddaughter's maid! Very well, Anna, I want to make amends for my dear Louise, I want you to learn to care for me, so, I will acquiesce to your wishes sufficiently to have that woman remain in the household as a parlour maid. I doubt she has the training, but I imagine that Patron will be able to teach her to serve coffee and gateaux in a tolerable way!'

Anna was wise enough to know that she must be satisfied with this.

'Thank you, Grandmere,' she said, getting to her feet, walking over to the elderly lady, and kissing her cheek. 'I assure you, you won't be sorry.'

Celestine looked at Anna sadly.

'Will I not? My dear, for once in my life I no longer know!'

Anna met her grandfather for the first time that afternoon.

Pierre summoned her to come to see him in his study.

After her experiences with her grandmother, Anna was quite apprehensive, as she tapped on the heavy, oaken door.

'Please come in,' said a surprisingly deep voice, in English.

Anna entered. At first, she didn't even see her grandfather, and looked around the large, beautifully furnished room in surprise. Where was he? And then he stood up, and walked around from behind the desk, and Anna realised why she hadn't at first noticed him.

Pierre de la Vigne was scarcely five foot tall, and very slimly built. Had he been taller, he would have been a handsome man, with his thick, unpowdered dark hair, and fine, aristocratic features.

'Please sit down, Granddaughter,' Pierre said, formally, indicating an ornate Louis XIV chair opposite his own.

Anna obeyed, without making any comment.

'I must apologise for not being with my wife to greet you when you first arrived, but I had been suffering with a migraine all day, and my physician advised me to rest.' He smiled engagingly.

'I know it sounds a poor excuse, but I have always suffered from migraine very badly, and in this instance I truly believe that it was brought on by the excitement of knowing that you were coming!'

Anna permitted herself a smile. She could see already that her grandmother was much the more dominant of the two, and yet Pierre had a certain Gallic charm which was quite endearing.

'I didn't expect either of you to be waiting up for me, Grandpere, after all, our arrival was very late!'

'Ah yes, I believe that you met with a member of the regrettable Dubois family.' He spread his hands helplessly. 'Those ruffians are particularly numerous in these parts, and I fear that the authorities are at a loss as to know how to deal with them! It is a sad state of affairs, is it not, Granddaughter, when the peasantry start to dictate to us.'

'Yes, I suppose it is,' Anna looked serious. 'Yet in my experience, the peasants, as you call them, have minds just as we have!'

'Ah ha! A liberated young lady! But then, ma cherie, I imagine that the awful experience that you have suffered has affected your thoughts to a degree.'

Anna inclined her head.

'Yes, sir, it has, it's made me think about things more. Before Newgate I tended to be somewhat selfish, thinking only of the next divertissement, but now I realise that there is much more to life that idle pleasure.' Then she laughed, a light, infectious sound. 'Oh, forgive me! I must sound a totally pompous prig!'

'On the contrary, Anna, my dear, you seem to me to be a most sensible young lady. For an old man like me, set in his ways, it is very difficult to comprehend that the peasantry are capable of thoughts like you or I, and yet I am sure that you have a point.

Possibly what they lack is opportunity and education, and yet these are radical thoughts.

'If we are to educate them too well, who knows where it will lead? Possibly to total anarchy and revolution!'

'Monsieur, I keep hearing talk of revolution. Tell me, do you think that France is on the verge of something as catastrophic as that?'

Pierre de la Vigne stared fixedly at a point a few feet above Anna's head for several moments, and, when he spoke, his voice was almost funereal.

'My dear child, I sincerely hope not, and yet I fear that it may very well come to that!' Then he looked directly at her, and smiled brightly. 'But let us not be so serious! Surely it is an occasion for rejoicing when one's granddaughter returns to her family! Tell me, Anna, dear, what think you of your cousin Julien?'

'Why do you ask?' she prevaricated, experiencing a shiver of distaste.

Pierre had the grace to look abashed.

'Well, child, he is the son of my first cousin, a dear fellow whom I was very fond of, and who was killed in action while serving under the Marquis de Lafayette. Julien has perhaps been a little spoilt by his mother, you see, he is an only child, but there is much good in the boy, which I am sure would become apparent were he to marry the right young lady . . . '

'I, too, sir, am an only child,' Anna replied, with some asperity, guessing where his remarks were leading. 'But, I assure you, after my sojourn in Newgate prison, I am anything but spoilt!'

'Exactly!' Pierre sat forward in his chair, and rubbed his hands together, his face a picture of enthusiasm. 'You would be perfect for Julien, ma chere!

'You have suffered, and you have experienced life from the other side of the blanket. To Julien, no-one is of any value unless he or she is a member of the upper classes, but you think differently, and could teach him a lot. He is a very handsome fellow, don't you think?'

Anna got to her feet, her expression like ice.

'No, grandfather, I do not consider that Julien is in the slightest bit handsome! To me, beauty comes from within, and at the risk of offending you, I am sorry to say that I do not feel that my cousin has a handsome soul! Now, if you will excuse me, I still have some unpacking to do!' And without waiting for his permission to retire, Anna turned towards the door.

'Wait!' The single word followed her.

Anna turned. She was trembling inside, knowing that she'd been quite rude about Julien, who was clearly a great favourite with her grandfather. And yet she hadn't been able to help herself.

'Yes, Grandfather?'

'You're a very insolent young lady who should thank her lucky stars that she doesn't live in Medieval times when she would have been flogged for her behaviour!' He shook his head sadly. 'And so like your mother, Louise, she wouldn't obey me either!'

'I'm sorry if I've offended you, Grandpere.' Anna replied, dropping a formal curtsey. 'Now, do I have your leave to retire?'

'Yes, you may as well go, my girl!' Pierre waved an imperious hand. 'Do you know, I had high hopes of you, but already, I fear that you've let me down!'

6

The remainder of the day wasn't too eventful — for which Anna was glad. She was still tired after the previous day's activities, and her reception from her grandparents had certainly been no better than she had expected.

All right, so Celestine had agreed to a compromise with respect to Meg, but even that had been hard won, and Anna had the unpleasant feeling that most of her dealings with her grandmother would be likely to follow the same mode.

As she had been warned, her grandmother was a strong, domineering character used to getting her own way, so she had expected the old woman to be a challenge, but she was somewhat dismayed by her interview with her grandfather.

She had been given to understand

that he was a meek little man, but he had introduced the subject of Julien very quickly, and had certainly been none-too-pleased with her own negative reaction.

These thoughts made unpleasant company, so she enquired where Meg had been put, and went to visit her that evening. Dinner, thankfully, had been a quiet affair, taken, at her choice, in her own room, both her grandparents and Julien at least seeming to appreciate the fact that she was feeling very tired.

Meg's quarters were certainly very different to her own, Anna reflected, with a trace of bitterness, as she made her way into the North wing, where the servants, with the exception of personal maids and manservants, were housed.

Meg's room was very small, and despite the oil lamp burning, gloomy.

Meg herself was lying in a rather uncomfortable looking iron bed, her head propped up on one solitary pillow. She looked pale and tired, and Anna's heart went out to her, especially when she saw the look of transparent pleasure which dawned in the older woman's deep blue eyes the moment they alighted on her.

'Mistress Anna, 'tis good to see you!' Then a look of worry passed over her thin face. 'But does the Mistress know that you're here? I doubt that she'll take kindly to her granddaughter visiting a mere servant!'

'My grandmother doesn't know, simply because I haven't bothered to tell her! But, believe me, Meg, it is something which she's going to have to get used to, for I will never abandon you after all you did for me!'

'You're a good girl, Mistress Anna, but I think that the Mistress feels that the likes of me is no fit companion for her granddaughter — her heiress, mark ye! And there, well, I fear she is right, for I'm not, am I?' And once again her raucous cackle of laughter sounded, ending in a spluttering cough.

'It's cold in here, Meg.' Anna glanced towards the fireplace. 'I shall order that a fire is made up, and you shall have more pillows. After all, you received a head wound, and you don't look comfortable lying flat down like that!'

'Now don't you go getting yourself into trouble on account of me, young lady! You've done quite enough for me already, getting me out of Newgate, and into a well-paid position! You yourself must admit that this room is real cosy compared to what we were used to in Newgate!'

'That's not the point!' Anna protested. 'You've been injured, and that wouldn't have happened if I hadn't dragged you off to France with me! No, Meg Skeels, I'm mistress now, and I am going to command them to bring you pillows and make up a fire!' Anna smiled impishly. 'Are there any more things that you need while I'm at it? Do you require some food and drink?'

Meg shook her head, then winced, clearly the wound was still paining her.

'I know, I'll have them bring you

some water and laudanum! What you need more than anything now is a good sleep! I won't stay on chattering to you now, for I'll likely make your poor head feel even worse!' So saying, she leaned down, and dropped a light kiss of Meg's cheek.

'Someone will be in to light the fire and bring the other things in a few moments. Rest well, Meg, and I'll see how you are tomorrow.'

'Goodnight, Mistress Anna, you're a good girl, but be warned by one who has more experience of life, don't overstep the mark on account of me!'

Anna made no answer, just pulled a face at Meg from the doorway, before going off in search of a servant to do her bidding.

That was accomplished quite easily, although Jacques was surprised by her request, and didn't bother to hide it. In fact, he looked her up and down quite insolently, as if weighing up whether he should bother to obey or not.

Anna found herself colouring under

his bold scrutiny, her satin-slippered foot tapping noiselessly on the stone floor.

'Well, what are you standing there gaping at?' she demanded, at length. 'I gave you an order! Are you dull-witted or something, that you do not obey it?'

'Actually,' Jacques sniggered. 'I am wondering whether I understood the young lady's French aright. You want me to go to that woman Meg's room and light a fire. Then you want pillows, laudanum and water for the likes of her?'

'Obviously, you have understood me perfectly,' Anna replied, irritably. She knew her French was far from perfect, but she'd deliberately spoken slowly, so that there shouldn't be any doubt of the servant being able to understand her.

'Well, 'tis certainly an unusual request in this place!' Jacques acknowledged. 'I take it that Madame knows nothing of this?'

'Do you question my orders?' Anna

snapped, hoping that her voice, and stance, was more authoritative than she actually felt.

'No, I'll be happy to do it, I just don't want no trouble, that's all!'

'You have the word of Miss Anna Heatherington for that!' Anna retorted, and fancied that she gleaned a dawning respect in the man's eyes as he touched his forelock and murmured. 'Right then, I'd best be getting along.'

Anna returned to her room, and prepared to get ready for bed. She was a little more shaken than she'd first thought. Clearly, the de la Vignes were not loved by their servants. But then, was that really so surprising?

Anna was up quite early the following day, and after her ablutions, rang for Charlotte, who slept in a smaller, adjoining room, to bring in her breakfast.

It was a beautiful, April morning, the sky blue and cloudless, and after a pleasant meal of croissants, Anna decided that she might as well go out and explore the chateau grounds.

It would be pleasant to get out, she reflected, as Charlotte insisted on helping her dress, for already the place was beginning to feel rather oppressive.

Anna opted for an outfit suitable for riding. She was a competent horsewoman, and although she hadn't actually been on a horse for some time, she was sure that it would soon all come back to her.

Charlotte wanted to accompany her, but Anna refused.

'No, Charlotte, I would appreciate some time alone.'

'But Madame will be horrified! Particularly if you go riding all on your own!'

Anna sighed, she could understand how Charlotte felt, and yet she refused to allow herself to be swayed by it.

'I haven't definitely decided whether I actually will go riding, but if I do, then I will take a groom with me. There now, does that satisfy you?'

'It isn't me, Mademoiselle Anna! It's

Madame! She is a very formidable lady! But yes, if I say that you have gone for a little walk in the grounds, perhaps to look at the stables, then she should not be too angry, although she will still think that I should have been there to chaperone you!'

'I'm not used to being constantly chaperoned! Tell her that I wouldn't let you, then she may begin to realise that there is more of her in me than perhaps she has thought!'

'That is a good idea, Mlle Anna!' Charlotte smiled. 'Although in truth, I think you are much the kinder!' And then, as if she feared that she had said too much, she began tidying away Anna's breakfast dishes.

She really had made rather an atrocious beginning by antagonising both her grandparents, Anna thought to herself, rather ruefully, as she went out into the chateau grounds and began walking in the direction of the stables.

Although the morning was quiet and still, Anna was so deeply involved in her unhappy thoughts, that she didn't notice Patrick riding towards her, and started visibly when he called to her.

'Hello, Anna! I was just coming to see you. How are things?' By this time, he had reined in his horse beside her, and dismounted.

'I'm sorry, I didn't mean to startle you!'

Anna shook her head, and smiled ruefully.

'No, it's my fault. I was lost in my own thoughts. Which aren't too happy, I'm afraid! Already, I seem to have alienated both my grandparents!'

Patrick shrugged, falling into step beside her and leading his horse along.

'I shouldn't think that would be too difficult! Do you want to tell me about it?'

Anna hesitated, gazing up at him. Then, all of a sudden, the temptation to talk became too much for her, and the words spilled out.

'They took too much upon themselves, your grandparents!' Patrick frowned darkly. 'Well, if you have any more problems regarding Meg, I would be very happy to employ her myself, I am in need of a good housekeeper!

'But as to your other problem, that, I fear, is a little more serious! I did wonder if Pierre would wish to marry you off to Julien, but I didn't expect him to start hinting about such things quite as soon as this!'

'Neither, Monsieur, did I!' Then she brightened. 'But perhaps I've been reading too much into his words, for, after all, I don't really know what Julien's feelings on the matter are!'

'Julien, I fear, will do almost anything if there is money involved! Oh, my dear, I do apologise, that probably sounds very rude, and I certainly didn't mean it to! Were it myself, then I would be very glad to have the opportunity of . . . ' He paused self-consciously, and Anna felt her heart begin to quicken. She was almost sure that Patrick had been about to mention marriage . . .

'But we are talking of Julien,' he

continued. 'I don't suppose you realise that he is very heavily in debt?'

'No, I hadn't realised!' Anna shook her head in surprise. 'To look at him, one would imagine that he is a wealthy gentleman!'

'An impression he is at pains to cultivate! In reality, I understand that the creditors are clamouring at his door! Your grandfather, on the other hand, is an extremely wealthy man.'

'Then, you think that if grandpere offers to settle money on me, he will wish us to marry?' Anna stopped in her tracks, her face anxious. 'Oh no, Patrick! I don't want to marry my cousin Julien! I don't even like him!'

Patrick let go of the horses' reins and drew her into his arms, his cheek nestling against hers.

'Oh Anna, Anna! Don't fret, my darling!' he murmured, his mouth close to hers. 'We'll find a way, don't you worry!'

Anna looked up at him, conscious of the beating of her heart as she did so.

Oh this was madness! But at that moment, she wanted nothing more than for him to kiss her . . .

But Patrick didn't. Instead he seemed to recollect himself, and put her gently from him, saying, in a voice that was not quite steady.

'Cesar is not the most patient of horses, as you see.'

Indeed, the big black stallion was pawing the ground impatiently.

'If I do not take hold of the reins and show him who is master, he will take it into that great, noble head of his to run off and leave me!'

Despite the tension of the past few minutes, Anna couldn't help but laugh.

'Then he must be a fool to even think of doing so!'

Patrick made no reply, but looked at her sharply. So, as he had allowed himself to hope, Anna wasn't indifferent to him. The knowledge filled his heart with joy. Then he sobered. There was no way that either of the de la Vignes would consider him a suitable match for their granddaughter. Their heiress.

Oh, he was comfortably enough off, wealthy, even. But his blood was by no means as blue as theirs. His father had been of the minor French nobility, but his mother, as they knew, had been but a penniless Irish gypsy. Certainly enough to condemn him in the eyes of a family who were most decidedly snobbish!

Anna was very much aware of Patrick's silence, and, unfortunately, misunderstood it.

She had been too forward. She had made no move to stop him when he had taken her into his arms, and then, to crown it all, she had told him that his horse would be a fool to think of leaving him! Oh, the shame of it all! What on earth must he think of her?

'There is no need for you to accompany me, you know,' she said, at length, a distinct chill having crept into her voice. 'I was on my way to the stables to look at the horses, and, if I find one with whom I have a rapport, then I will go out for a ride.'

'I had guessed that was where you were heading.' His voice was mild. 'And, if I may be so bold, should you find a horse with whom you feel a rapport, and I should think you will, the de la Vigne stables boasting some forty or so animals, then I would deem it a great honour if you would permit me to ride with you.

'I could show you something of the countryside, and, I fancy, it would also be safer for you to have a male companion in times such as these!'

Anna had been about to turn down his offer, but his last words stopped her, and, instead, she looked anxious.

'You mean that the Dubois might be sufficiently bold to strike in daytime?'

'There have been isolated attacks on various prominent citizens in the region, two of them in daylight. The offenders have never been brought to justice, although rumour is quite positive in placing them as the clan Dubois.'

'But how do they get away with it?'

Anna wanted to know. 'If they were in England, they would speedily be gracing the branches of Tyburn tree!'

'But they are not in England, are they?' Patrick replied, with a shrug of his shoulders. 'And France, as I have tried to warn your family on numerous occasions, is no longer as it used to be! It is a country which is teetering on the verge of revolution. Law and order is breaking down with appalling rapidity, and yet people like your grandparents and Julien refuse to see it!'

'My grandmother is aware that times are changing,' Anna replied, thoughtfully. 'She said something of that nature to me.' Then she rounded on Patrick almost accusingly. 'But what would you have them do? Surely you do not support the Dubois as opposed to my grandparents!'

'I see, dear Anna, that Newgate has done little to change you! You are still an aristocrat at heart!' Patrick remarked cynically.

'Dr St Clair, that was unfair!' Anna

glared at him quite ferociously.

'I know, Mademoiselle, and I apologise! Nevertheless, I wanted you to be aware of the fact that aristocrats like your family are not omnipotent. The Dubois have acted in a violent way, and yet, there are some, no, there are many, of the ordinary people who are coming to feel that they have had no choice!

'They are a large peasant family who, over the centuries, have suffered great wrongs. Well, I suppose that there is nothing strange in that, many families have, in France and elsewhere. The Dubois, however, seem to me to have received even more persecution in recent times.' He smiled, 'I have no wish to sound like a mouldy old text book, yet I have made it a hobby of mine to study French history.' He looked at Anna keenly. 'I'm not boring you, I trust.'

'Not at all, Please continue, I would learn something of my mother country.'

'Very well. Although you may not

like all that you hear! The persecution of the Dubois seems to have been a favourite pastime of your great-grandfather, Raoul de la Vigne, who used to make a habit of demanding the rights of Droit de Seigneur with Dubois ladies, whether they were married or not!'

'He doesn't sound a very pleasant person, but then, I have the suspicion that my ancestors probably were not!'

'Don't take it too personally!' Patrick gave her a fond smile. 'French aristocrats have done what they wanted for centuries, which is probably why the peasants are at last rebelling today! But to go back to my story.

'Unfortunately, Raoul didn't just demand these rights. He was also devilishly severe on poachers, and when a Dubois husband dared to complain about his attentions to his wife, he had the poor fellow convicted on a trumped-up charge and broken on the wheel!'

'He must have been a monster,

and I'm his great-granddaughter! Oh, Patrick! Small wonder that you don't like me!'

Patrick St Clair looked at her with sad, dark eyes.

'My dear Anna, that is simply not true! If you want truth, then I like you far, far too well!'

7

By this time, they had reached the stables, so Anna was spared from answering.

She was very glad, because, what could she have said? She knew by now that she was at least half-way to falling in love with Patrick St Clair. Probably more. To hear him say that he cared for her was music to her ears. And yet, at the same time, it also disturbed and worried her.

Her grandfather wanted her to marry Julien, and, apparently, although she hadn't yet said anything to Anna herself, her grandmother wanted her to marry the as yet unknown to Anna, Antoine de Mandeville. Would they allow her to marry Patrick, that is, if he wanted to marry her? Anna doubted it . . .

Of course, should it come to that,

she could always elope like her mother, Louise, had done . . .

'Bonjour, Gaston,' Patrick greeted a tall, wiry-looking man.

The man's somewhat sullen face was immediately transformed into a pleasant smile, Anna noticed, with surprise, and realised that Patrick was popular with the de la Vigne servants, or, at least, with this one.

'Bonjour Monsieur le docteur. How are you?' His dark eyes took stock of Anna. 'And who is the young lady? Are you courting, Monsieur?'

Patrick threw back his head and laughed.

'Chance would be a fine thing, mon ami! No, the lady you see with me is the long-lost granddaughter of the de la Vignes. Mademoiselle Louise's daughter. Gaston, let me introduce you to Miss Anna Heatherington!'

It was a theatrical introduction, and Anna found herself blushing under Gaston's scrutiny. What would be his reaction? Would he immediately hate

143

her because she was a de la Vigne?

But no, Gaston was actually smiling, as he bowed to her.

'Mademoiselle Louise's daughter, why, I should have known! She's a ringer for her, is she not, Monsieur? Mademoiselle Anna, I will serve you with all my heart, as I did your dear mother, God rest her soul!'

She took hold of his hand, intending to shake it, but he raised it to his lips.

'Your mother was a saint, bless her, not like . . . ' He broke off, fear evident in his dark eyes. 'Oh, Mademoiselle, I didn't mean any harm, I . . . '

'Gaston, please don't upset yourself. To me you seem like a really kind man, and I am flattered that you intend to serve me as you did my mother. And now I would like to go riding. Have you got a suitable horse, do you think?'

'Bless you, Mademoiselle!' Gaston smiled. 'Yes, I am sure that I have just the mount for you. Her name is Fifi, and she is a spirited mare of some six years. Perhaps you would care to follow me and come and look at her?'

Anna smiled back at him.

'Thank you, Gaston, there's nothing that I would like more!' And she and Patrick followed him into the stables.

Fifi was a spritely little white mare, and Anna fell in love with her immediately. The horse seemed to sense Anna's feelings, and nuzzled her soft, velvet nose against Anna's hand.

'Oh, she's beautiful!' Anna exclaimed, enthusiastically. 'Thank you for thinking of her for me, Gaston, you couldn't have chosen a horse which would have suited me any better!'

'If she were mine, Mam'selle, then I would give her to you, but alas, she is the property of your grandmere. Still, Madame Celestine may decide to make you a present of her when she realises how much you like Fifi.'

'Well, I suppose I could always try! Still, I will be quite content just so long as she allows me to ride Fifi.'

Gaston looked momentarily disconcerted.

'Does Madame not know that you are going riding this morning?'

It was Patrick who answered, for which Anna was grateful, as she had no wish to lie directly to the kindly stableman.

'I'll be accompanying Miss Anna on Cesar, so you needn't worry, Gaston, I'll make sure that she comes to no harm.'

'Monsieur Patrick is an expert horseman, you will be in very good hands with him, Mam'selle! Right, I will saddle up Fifi for you, as I expect that you're anxious to get off on your way. It's a beautiful spring morning, isn't it?'

He chatted to them as he worked, his dark hands deft and skilful. Then he led Fifi out into the morning sunshine, where Cesar was standing tethered to a post, a look of haughty impatience on his handsome, arrogant face.

Gaston threw back his head and laughed.

'Monsieur Cesar is not pleased by the delay! I warrant, Monsieur, that he will give you quite a run for your money!'

'Yes,' he agreed. 'It rather looks that way, doesn't it?' As he spoke, he released Cesar from the post, and handed his reins to Gaston, while he helped Anna to mount Fifi.

Anna was, of course, obliged to ride side-saddle, something which she found rather irksome. When her father had still possessed a country home, before the bailiffs had stepped in and reclaimed it due to his mounting gambling debts, she had frequently been in the habit of riding astride her horse, if she was in a secluded place.

They cantered through the chateau's grounds, and Anna found that although she hadn't been on a horse for quite sometime, she still felt at home in the saddle, as she had done as a child and while she was in her early teens.

'You look as if you and the horse are as one.' Patrick remarked, giving her an admiring look. 'Obviously you're well used to riding.' Then he gave her an impish smile. 'Mind you, I would warrant a guess that you're not too happy riding side-saddle, and, I must say that I do not blame you!

'It's a very stupid restriction, to my way of thinking, and, if you would prefer, once we get away from the chateau grounds, you can ride astride Fifi, that way you'll probably enjoy yourself much better!'

'I have to confess that I am much more used to riding that way! I like the freedom, and I find that it's much more practical if one wants to give the horse exercise, and allow him or her to gallop.'

'Which is what old Cesar will want!' Patrick exclaimed as the horse made a valiant effort to surge forward, and had to be forcibly restrained. 'All right, old boy, calm down,' he crooned into the horse's ear. 'You'll get your gallop, but have patience, wait until we're clear of here and into the wood.'

Cesar's head seemed to shoot up, his expression crafty and knowing.

'You know, if I didn't know better, I could have sworn that Cesar understood every word you said!' Anna remarked.

'Oh, but he did! Didn't you, old chap? You see, Anna, this lad and I have been together for quite a long time, my late father gave him to me on my sixth birthday.' He shook his head, a rueful grin playing around his mouth.

'Not really the most suitable of presents for a youngster of that age, I certainly took a tumble or two! But then Cesar and I gained a respect for one another. Well, I'm just turned thirty now, so we've been together twenty-four years, when all's said and done!'

'And what age is Cesar?'

'Oh, a little younger than me! He

was a two year old when my father gave him to me, which makes him twenty six.'

'He's a good deal older than Fifi, then. Didn't Gaston say that she was six?'

'Yes, I believe so.' Patrick looked amused. 'But why does it concern you, Anna? You're not thinking of a match for them are you?'

'No, I think not! They hardly seem the ideal couple, after all! He's so dark, and Fifi so light-coloured. Then he's tall, and she's petite, and even their eye colours, his are dark, whereas Fifi's seem to be almost emerald and . . .'

She broke off, her hand going involuntarily to her mouth, as she suddenly realised that the description of the horses was sounding increasingly like a description of Patrick and herself . . .

He read her thoughts.

'And then there's the age difference,' he murmured. 'A little much, perhaps, in the case of Fifi and Cesar, yet not,

I think, perhaps in our case. How old are you, Anna? About eighteen?'

Anna's heart was beating painfully against the confines of her riding outfit.

'I'm nineteen,' she murmured, her voice not quite steady.

'A suitable age for marriage.' By this time, they were approaching the wood, and he drew Cesar to a reluctant halt, and slid off his back. 'Let me assist you to dismount, and then you can cease riding side-saddle and we can give the horses some real exercise.'

His tone had become quite curt, peremptory, even, and Anna felt hurt by his sudden change of mood. After all, how could she know that he was thinking that, at nineteen, the de la Vignes would no doubt be anxious to marry her off as soon as possible, and to a suitable parti . . .

'There's no need for you to help me!' she exclaimed, tartly, slipping nimbly to the ground without giving him an opportunity of aiding her. She didn't want to feel his arms around her, she found it curiously disconcerting . . .

'As you wish,' he replied formally, and re-mounted Cesar while she climbed back up onto Fifi, her divided riding skirt eminently suitable for riding astride.

'Ready?' he enquired, one dark eyebrow raised almost sardonically.

'Of course! Although I doubt my little mare will be able to keep up with your stallion, I'm sure she'll give you a fair run for your money!'

'Don't try to force Fifi to go faster than she wants to,' he replied, his voice severe. 'It's a long time since you've ridden, and I don't want anything to happen to you. After all, you're in my charge!'

Nothing about really caring about her, Anna noted, grimly. Just that he felt responsible for her, almost like a guardian. Well, she'd show him!

Leaning forward in the saddle, she murmured words of encouragement in the little mare's ears, and then they were off, Fifi's hooves kicking up dust as she sped through the forest at breakneck speed.

'Anna, wait!' Patrick called, from behind her. 'There's some uneven terrain around here, and you don't know the area, you could be thrown!'

But Anna wasn't listening to him, she was enjoying herself too much . . .

If she'd have been thinking rationally, Anna would have realised that it wouldn't last. But she wasn't, she was curiously exhilarated by her sudden burst of freedom after the confines of Newgate, and, in a different way, the restrictions of the de la Vigne chateau.

It didn't take Patrick long to reach her, however. Cesar was a much more powerful horse, and as Fifi suddenly stumbled slightly on an uneven patch of ground, Anna felt the mare's bridle being grasped, and the next moment they were pulled up to an unceremonious halt, Anna sliding forward in the saddle, and almost going over the mare's head.

'You silly girl!' Patrick's face was

dark with fury. 'Why on earth did you go dashing off like that, you could have killed yourself!'

'It wasn't my fault, you great bully!' Anna responded, angrily. 'After all, it was you who suddenly caught hold of Fifi's bridle and brought her to such an abrupt halt that I could well have been thrown!'

'There was no chance of that, Fifi had already slowed down when she stumbled on that clump of earth! On the other hand, left to your own devices, you would undoubtedly have fallen. As I tried to tell you, you don't know the wood, and, believe me, there are numerous pitfalls in it, such as traps for game, and even the occasional fallen branch.' The anger had left him now, though, and instead his face looked anxious.

'Oh, Anna, my love! Why did you want to get away from me like that? Surely I have done nothing to offend you?'

And how could she answer that?

How could she tell him that he had offended her by his sudden change of mood. He had appeared almost lover-like, and then he had acted as if she was but a wilful child, whom he had the misfortune to chaperone.

'Of course you haven't offended me!' she snapped, shortly. 'Why don't we stop trying to analyse things and get on with our ride?'

He looked at her curiously, but made no comment other than, 'Of course, if that's what you wish, but this time I will lead the way, and you will follow!' And he led Cesar in front, and began cantering along at a fair, but not fast, pace.

Anna was seething. How dare he say that he would lead and her follow! Just who did he think she was, to be spoken to in such a way!

'I think I can at least manage to ride alongside you, sir,' she remarked, with mock deference, fitting the mare's paces to Cesar's.

'No doubt you can!' he replied with

a lazy grin. 'All right then, Anna, let's give them a gallop, but please, keep Fifi a pace or two behind.'

'Very well, since you put it in a polite and rational way, then I shall.'

Patrick looked amused. She was a spirited little thing, which only served to endear her to him all the more. She deserved much better than Julien de la Vigne . . .

Anna enjoyed the remainder of the ride very much. Patrick stopped in a beautiful little hollow, and tethered the horses to an aged oak tree, while they went for a walk.

'It's lovely in here, so peaceful!' Anna exclaimed.

'Yes, I used to spend quite a lot of time here when I was a boy.' His voice grew reminiscent. 'Whenever there were any problems at home, and, believe me, there were plenty, my parents were a very, er shall we say, spirited couple? Anyway, when they'd been arguing, I would come out into the woods here.'

Anna found that she could picture Patrick as a boy. Even then, she was sure that he would be sensitive, easily hurt. So very different from Julien . . .

Without being aware that she'd done so, Anna shuddered.

'My dear, you're not cold, are you?' Patrick asked, his arm going around her slender shoulders.

'No, it wasn't because I was feeling cold, it was just my thoughts which were troubling me.'

'Which were?' he asked, immediately.

'I was thinking about Julien,' she said, after a momentary hesitation.

'Then you do have some feelings for him after all.'

'Oh yes, I think I do! Unfortunately, though, they are not kindly ones!' She looked perplexed. 'It's strange, really, Julien has been perfectly civil towards me, and yet I just cannot bring myself to like him.'

'Would it help any if I said that I don't care for him either?'

Anna turned towards him and smiled.

'Oh yes, I forgot for a moment that the two of you aren't really friends, and only developed a kind of friendship because you saved him from drowning!'

'Well, if I hadn't, it would have been on my conscience! Ah, now we're approaching the stream by which I used to meditate . . . Perhaps a few minutes here, Anna, and then, I suppose we should be returning. By this time, I should imagine that your grandparents may well have discovered that their chick has fled the nest . . . '

8

It was after eleven when Anna returned to the chateau, and her absence had, indeed, been noticed.

'Oh, thank goodness you're back, Mademoiselle!' a servant exclaimed. 'You are to join Madame with Monsieur le Duc de Mandeville in the Pompadour room immediately.'

Anna sighed. The last thing she felt like was meeting the man who had been her mother's suitor, and now, presumably, had come to pay court to her!

'Thank you,' she said aloud to the servant. 'I hope I haven't caused you to wait here for me for long? I didn't mean to be so long.'

'No, of course not, Mam'selle. Now, would you like me to show you the way to the Pompadour room?'

'Well, if I'm to find it, I think you'll

have to! Just a moment, though, I'd better go to the cloakroom first and straighten my hair.'

'If I may help you, Mam'selle?' The servant asked timidly.

'You certainly may!' Anna said gratefully 'What is your name, anyway?'

'Marie Lapin, Mam'selle,' the girl replied, as she deftly fixed the remaining pins more securely in Anna's silky, blonde hair. 'I am no expert at hair styling, but I think that looks a little more presentable, Mam'selle.'

'It does indeed,' Anna replied. 'Oh well, I suppose I'd best be on my way. Tell me, Marie, is my grandmother angry with me?'

'She was not too pleased when she discovered you were missing, particularly as she was expecting Monsieur le Duc,'

'Oh, was she indeed? Then I'm glad that I was!'

'Monsieur le Duc is a very fine gentleman.'

'Nevertheless, I do not like plans

made behind my back!'

Marie made no answer, and they continued down the corridor in silence, Marie stopping in front of a door on the right.

'Is this it?' Anna wanted to know.

Marie nodded.

'All right, you can go now. Thank you for you help.'

Marie dropped a curtsey, and hurried back along the corridor.

Anna knocked on the door, and her grandmother's voice bid her to enter.

Celestine and Antoine de Mandeville were sitting in armchairs either side of the fireplace, in which burned a fire, despite the warmth of the spring morning.

As Anna entered, Antoine de Mandeville rose to his feet, and crossed the room towards her.

Anna remained where she was and took the opportunity of studying him.

He was a tall, thin, slightly stooped man whom she judged to be around her father's age of forty-eight. He was soberly dressed, and yet his clothes were excellently cut, and clearly expensive.

His features were regular, although his nose was slightly long. When he smiled, however, his plain face was transformed into being almost handsome.

He was only a few feet away from Anna, when he suddenly stopped, one hand clutching at his heart, the other going to his forehead, which, Anna noticed, was perspiring beneath the white, powdered wig which he wore.

'Nom de Dieu!' he exclaimed. 'But it is Louise! You have come back to me!'

And before Anna had a chance to make any move at all, she found herself swept off her feet and into Antoine de Mandeville's arms.

'Antoine!' Her grandmother's peremptory voice cut through the air like a whip. 'Put her down at once! She is not Louise! Louise is dead! She is my granddaughter, Anna Heatherington, and although she resembles Louise, you will note that her colouring is really quite different!'

Antoine de Mandeville released her immediately, his rather pale face turning red. He reached for Anna's hand, and brought it to his lips.

'Oh, my dear! I am so very, very sorry! It is just that I have dreamed of seeing Louise again for so many years, and then, when you walked into the room, well, my emotions overcame my commonsense! I do hope that you can find it in your heart to forgive an old man's foolishness?'

Anna smiled, feeling sorry for him.

'Of course I forgive you!' she replied, truthfully.

'Well, that is more than I do for you, you wicked chit of a girl!' Her grandmother tutted 'Just where have you been all morning?'

'I've been out!' she said, shortly.

Antoine de Mandeville stepped into the frozen silence which followed.

'My dear Mam'selle Anna, will you do me the honour of sitting and talking with me? I am so very pleased to meet you!'

'Of course I will.' Anna replied, taking his arm and allowing him to lead her over to yet another ornate armchair which was placed in the vicinity of the blazing fire.

It was uncomfortably hot and stuffy, and Anna found herself wishing that she'd stayed out longer.

Her grandmother continued to regard her with disapproval, and Antoine de Mandeville with a kind of slavish devotion which, while she felt pity for him, she also found highly disconcerting.

She felt sure that in his mind, he was still seeing her as her mother, returned to him after all these years. That he would wish to marry her, she didn't doubt. And she hadn't realised that he was a Duc. She felt sure that her grandmother would move heaven and earth to see her only grandchild a Duchess . . .

Antoine de Mandeville had been invited to stay for lunch, which was a formal affair, held in the grand dining room.

Pierre and Julien were also present, neither saying much to Antoine, and Anna rightly surmised that they both resented his presence.

The meal seemed to last for hours. Anna hardly ate anything, for although she'd had an appetite when she'd first come in from her ride, the Duc's unwelcome presence had quite made her lose it.

He continued to praise her lavishly, and when she did speak, which was as little as possible, he hung on every word she said.

Celestine, at the head of the huge dining table, had at last thawed out towards Anna, and was watching benignly.

At last, Pierre got to his feet.

'Let's retire to my study for a glass of port, eh, Julien?' Julien stood up gratefully. He, too, had been finding the meal something of a strain.

De Mandeville was a thorn in his

flesh. He was deeply in debt, and it would solve his financial problems if he married Anna. De Mandeville, on the other hand, was fabulously rich. Would Pierre, influenced by Celestine, change his mind and decide that his granddaughter would be better marrying the Duc?

'De Mandeville,' Pierre was saying. 'You will, of course, join us.'

Antoine looked as if he would much prefer to stay with Anna, but he was sufficiently well-bred to know that the formalities must be obeyed, so he got to his feet, and with a bow to Anna, followed the two other men out of the room.

'You have made quite a conquest, Granddaughter!' Celestine observed, her thin lips breaking into a smile, once the gentlemen had left the room.

'Not I,' Anna replied, evenly. 'Rather, I think, the ghost of Louise!'

'How dare you! You are a most ungrateful girl! Don't you realise that the Duc is enormously wealthy, and will make you an excellent husband?'

'I don't care if he's the wealthiest man on earth — he's old, and I don't want to marry him!'

'Huh! You foolish girl! I suppose, like your poor mother, you would marry for love! Well, who is he? Have you already found the man that you would marry?'

'No . . . no, of course not!' Anna replied quickly.

'Hmm . . . Somehow, I think differently! Well, Granddaughter, I will just have to watch, and wait for you to give yourself away, won't I?'

Which meant that Anna had to be very careful, for she had no wish for her grandmother to suspect that she had fallen in love with Patrick St Clair.

Patrick was a frequent visitor over the next week, ostensibly to see how Meg and the coachman were faring, but Anna hoped, also to see her.

Celestine had given Anna permission to ride Fifi, and she did this daily. She was not, however, permitted to ride alone, both her grandparents maintaining that it was unsafe in these difficult times, so sometimes she rode with Patrick, Julien unfortunately deciding to accompany them, and once, at her grandmother's instigation, with Antoine de Mandeville.

Anna had insisted that her maid, Charlotte, accompany her when she rode with de Mandeville. He was so much in love with Louise's memory, that she didn't feel that she could trust him . . .

As it was, he contrived to out-ride the maidservant, who was uncertain on a horse, and asked Anna if she would consider becoming his wife.

'Monsieur le Duc, I have no desire to marry yet,' Anna had replied, in as steady a voice as she could muster. 'I know that at nineteen I should, perhaps, be thinking of marriage, yet I do not feel that I am ready to.'

'I've rushed you. I should not have spoken so soon,' he replied, with a pent-up sigh. 'It's just that you're so beautiful, and I'm so much in love with you! Oh, Anna, at least give me leave to court you!'

Fortunately, at that moment, Charlotte caught up with them, and Anna was spared from answering. Nevertheless, she was unnerved, and swore to keep out of Antoine de Mandeville's way as much as possible . . .

Julien, on the other hand, didn't make a direct proposal. Once again, Anna tried to avoid being alone with him if she possibly could, but sometimes it was rather difficult when they lived in the same place!

One wet morning, she went to the library in search of something to read.

She was engrossed in browsing through the books, and didn't hear the door open, or see her cousin, until suddenly everything went dark, Julien having put his hands over her eyes.

'What . . . Who's that?' she cried out, startled.

Julien took his hands away and spun her round to face him.

'Who indeed but your devoted cousin! What are you reading, my princess? Hmm . . . Macbeth! You are a fan of Shakespeare's?' As he spoke, he sat down on one of the chairs next to the table, drawing Anna down to sit beside him.

'I like a number of his plays,' Anna replied, guardedly. 'Macbeth, I think, is my favourite..'

'A dark tale of passion and murder,' Julien replied, succinctly. 'Are you passionate, my Anna?' As he spoke, his hand reached out, drawing her reluctant hand into his.

'No, I'm not!' She reached out for the book which Julien had placed on the table. 'And now, if you'll excuse me, I'll take my book and go and read it!'

'Are you frightened of me, Anna?' Julien was right behind her, as she made for the door.

'Frightened of you? Of course not! Why should I be?'

'You know that your grandfather

wants us to marry, don't you? And the thought isn't pleasing to you, is it?' As he spoke, he reached out, caught a strand of her hair and curled it around his finger, so that she was, in affect, his prisoner . . . 'And you know why it isn't pleasing to you?'

He paused, waiting for her answer. Anna said nothing, just gazed at him like a rabbit hypnotised by a stoat . . .

'I can see you're not going to tell me. Very well, then I'll tell you. The reason that you do not wish to marry me is because you harbour fantasies of marrying Patrick St Clair!' He threw back his head and laughed.

'Grow up, Anna! Can you really imagine your proud grandparents allowing their heiress to marry a mere doctor?'

Anna jerked violently, and Julien released the strand of hair.

As she stumbled through the doorway, his hateful laugh followed her . . .

9

There was a vicious streak in Julien's character, Anna was sure of it, and she resolved to keep out of his way unless there was someone else present.

Fortunately, he had to go away to attend to some business in Nantes, which helped a lot, although he would return for the grand Easter ball, which, Celestine told Anna, was to be held in the chateau ballroom. It was to be a masked ball, and all the neighbouring gentry had been invited.

Anna might have been excited about it, only she was horribly aware of the constant bickering between her grandparents.

Celestine wanted there to be an announcement of a formal betrothal between Anna and Antoine, whereas Pierre wished to use the occasion to announce the engagement of Anna to Julien.

The only good thing was that no settlement could be reached, so it seemed highly unlikely that an announcement of any kind could be achieved.

Antoine was, however, a very frequent visitor to the chateau now, delighting in Julien's absence, and doing his utmost to seek out Anna whenever he could.

Celestine, of course, encouraged him, but Anna had an ally in her grandfather, who was more than happy to keep the couple apart.

Fortunately, Pierre seemed to be totally unaware of the growing feelings between Anna and Patrick St Clair, so Anna was able to ride with Patrick quite often, her grandfather happy to give her permission to do so.

Anna hadn't realised it, but Celestine was starting to become suspicious, and on the eve of the Easter ball, she summoned Anna to her bedchamber.

'Are you sure I'm not disturbing you,

Grandmere? You look quite tired.'

'Nonsense, child! I am simply taking things easy today so that I shall be in fine fettle for the ball tomorrow! You are looking forward to it, I trust? Come and sit down here, I would talk with you.'

'Yes, the ball sounds a very grand affair,' Anna replied, guardedly, wondering what the conversation was leading up to.

'Alas, your cousin Julien is returning today, and I could wish he wasn't!'

Here, Anna agreed with her, but made no comment.

'He is a ne'er do well, that young man, and would never make you happy, even if he has taken in your grandfather!' She eyed Anna keenly. 'Tell me, do you harbour any feelings for Julien? After all, he is a handsome enough young man, and nearner to your own age than Monsieur le Duc de Mandeville.'

'I don't harbour any kindly feelings towards him.' Anna replied.

'That is good to hear!' Celestine smiled. 'I didn't think that you did, but felt it was better to make sure. Well then, why is it that you do not appear to favour Antoine? Is it just that he is a number of years older than you?'

'Monsieur le Duc is very kind.' Anna sighed heavily to herself. 'But I cannot help but feel that he is more in love with my mother's memory than he is with me! Also, I would prefer to marry someone who was nearer to my own age.'

'And you have someone in mind?' Celestine noticed Anna's hesitation. 'You do, don't you? And I have a suspicion that I know who he is. Patrick St Clair.'

Anna made no answer, but tell-tale colour flooded her cheeks.

'So, I am right! Well, child, don't distress yourself, for I am not going to get angry, I am just going to tell you that it just will not do! You are our sole heiress, you come from an extremely noble, and wealthy family. I have nothing against Patrick St Clair. In fact, believe it or not, I quite admire the fellow! But, Anna, you must surely see that he is just not in your league!'

Her grandmother was, in way, echoing Julien's words. And yet it was all so stupid! Louise was from a noble family, but Anna's late father, although educated, had proved himself to be hopelessly irresponsible. A wastrel.

If he hadn't persistently gambled, he probably wouldn't have been killed in a duel, and Anna herself wouldn't have ended up in Newgate prison!

'You look thoughtful,' Celestine said. 'May I be a party to your thoughts?'

'No, Grandmere, I'm sorry, but I'm just not ready to share them.' She bent down and kissed the paper thin cheek. 'I will think upon what you have said.'

And then, without giving her a chance to answer, she hurried from the room.

Anna's emotions were mixed as

Charlotte helped her prepare for the ball.

Her costume was that of a shepherdess — not, in Anna's opinion, very original, but it had been her grandmother's choice.

Charlotte, however, was wildly enthusiastic, and declared that 'Mam'selle Anna was absolutely ravishing!'

Her hair had been arranged by a stylist brought in especially for the occasion. A make-up artist had then skilfully applied powder and rouge to Anna's cheeks, with a crescent star patch on one cheek, the only patch she would allow, as she really didn't care for such things.

'I don't look like me,' she said aloud.

'But surely that is the idea, Mam'selle!' Charlotte smiled. 'After all, it is a masked, fancy dress ball, the masks only being removed at midnight.'

Anna supposed that Charlotte had a point. Certainly, she had no desire to be recognised by Antoine de Mandeville or her cousin Julien!

'And I'm to carry this little crook as well!' Anna gave a chuckle. 'It's a wonder there isn't an imitation sheep to go with it!'

'Oh, Mam'selle Anna! Why are you being such a cynic? Didn't you have any masked balls when you were living in England?'

'No,' Anna replied, shortly, not bothering to elaborate on the fact that due to her father's steady gambling, there wouldn't have been any money for them! Then she relented when she saw how disappointed Charlotte was looking.

'I think I'm just a trifle nervous, Charlotte, never having been to such a gathering before. Tell me, will there be many people there?'

'There are always quite a number of people at a ball held by the de la Vignes. It is considered a great honour to receive an invitation! On this occasion, it would not surprise me if there were even more than usual. Your grandparents will be anxious to show you off.' She stood back, surveying her mistress.

'And, if I may be as bold to say so, with good cause! You will certainly be the most beautiful lady in the room!'

'Thank you, Charlotte! You've done my self-confidence a power of good!'

That evening, Anna entered the ballroom with her grandfather, who was in the garb of a sultan. Celestine, resplendent in a costume to represent Diana, the goddess of the Moon, was already there, welcoming the guests.

And a motley assortment they were, Anna reflected, as her eyes took in a Cossack, a monk, a Roman emperor, various gods and goddesses, a person dressed in a costume which depicted the Ace of Spades, and many other costumes which she could not, right away, put a name to.

Everyone was masked, for which Anna was thankful. Nevertheless, she immediately noticed Antoine de

Mandeville, dressed in a Harlequin type costume, talking to a lady who might, or might not, have been Venus.

Anna looked away. She had no wish for de Mandeville to see her.

'Ma cherie,' Pierre was saying. 'Let me escort you to your grandmother, and then I will fetch you something to drink. What would you like?'

'I'll have a glass of Madeira, please, Grandpere,' Anna replied, allowing him to take her arm and escort her towards Celestine, who, thankfully, was seated in the opposite direction to where the Duc was standing.

Of Julien, Anna had as yet seen no sign. But there again, the ballroom was already quite full, with several couples dancing a minuet, so it was possible that she hadn't noticed him. Or perhaps his costume was so convincing that she hadn't recognised him.

'Ah, Anna, ma chere!' Celestine exclaimed, catching sight of her granddaughter. She waved an imperious hand at a servant. 'Fetch an additional chair for my granddaughter. I would have her sit with me!'

The servant bowed, and hastened to do her bidding.

Celestine smiled at the couple she had just been welcoming.

'Anna, pray let me introduce you to Antony and Cleopatra. I assure you they are very good neighbours of ours, but I shall say no more until the hour of unmasking arrives!'

Which was somewhat unfair, Anna reflected, seeing as the couple were well aware of her identity! Still, obviously it was not a prerequisite of the ball for the de la Vignes to be unrecognised, only their guests . . .

Meanwhile, 'Antony' was bowing to her, while 'Cleopatra' curtsied.

'We are very happy to make your acquaintance,' Antony said, and Anna curtsied and extended her hand, which he touched with his lips. 'She is very beautiful, is she not?' he remarked, turning to Celestine.

Celestine looked at Anna proudly,

and Anna realised, with surprise, that there was also affection in the older woman's eyes.

'I think so! In fact, in this costume, she is quite ravishing.'

'You flatter me, I think, Grandmere!' Anna responded, as Pierre approached them, bringing Anna's Madeira, and carrying a glass of port for himself.

Antony and Cleopatra departed, and an elderly gentleman, dressed as a wizard, took their place.

Anna found that she was introduced to a number of people, or rather, they were introduced to her, as she didn't learn their names. Then she felt a slight tap on her arm, and turning, looked into the eyes of Antoine de Mandeville, shining blue beneath his black, satin mask.

'Mam'selle shepherdess, would you do me the honour of allowing me to dance with you?'

'Anna would love to!' Celestine replied, without giving Anna the opportunity of replying. 'Off you go, my love, and enjoy yourself! After all, it can give you no great pleasure just sitting here with an old woman!'

'But I'm quite happy here!' Anna responded.

'Nonsense! Off you go, girl, I would watch you dance!'

And so Anna had no choice. Fortunately, the dance was a fast polka, so there was no time for any conversation.

When it was finished, Antoine suggested they go and sit in one of the alcoves, and he would bring refreshments and they could talk in peace.

'No, I'm sorry, Monsieur.' Anna shook her head. 'I think that my grandmother wishes me to remain with her so that she can present me to her guests.' Actually, Anna was quite sure that Celestine would much rather if she stayed with Antoine, but she wasn't going to tell him that!

As it was, he seemed to accept her excuse, and after bowing to her formally, assured her that he would be over very soon to claim her for another dance.

'And now I will lead you back to your grandmere.' And he took Anna's arm in order to escort her back to her seat.

They had only taken a couple of steps, however, when a peremptory voice said, 'There's no need to escort Anna back to her seat, de Mandeville!' Then came that hateful laugh. 'Ah, yes, I can see through your little disguise!' And then Julien turned to Anna, and extended his arm. 'Come, cousin, I would dance with you!'

'Well, maybe you would, but I have no wish to dance with you!' Anna retorted. Julien was dressed as a cavalier, with a long, black periwig and plumed hat. Small wonder that she hadn't recognised him. 'Monsieur le Duc, kindly escort me back to Grandmere!'

But Julien wasn't prepared to give in so easily.

'Anna, I think you had better come and dance with me.' His voice was deceptively silky. 'I assure you, I have your grandfather's permission!'

Anna looked daggers at him, but she was sensible enough to realise that what he said was probably true, and she had no wish to cause a scene in public.

'Very well, although I think you will find my knowledge of the Gavotte sadly lacking!' She turned to de Mandeville and curtsied. 'Monsieur.'

'If you do not wish to dance, cousin dear, then we can leave the ballroom and sample the night air. After all, as I'm sure you will agree, it is a most pleasant evening . . . '

'I would as soon be alone with a poisonous snake as alone with you!' Anna retorted. 'No, Monsieur, let us dance.'

Anna had not altogether been joking when she had said that her knowledge of the Gavotte was scant. She did, however, exaggerate her clumsiness, taking great pleasure in treading on

Julien's toes on several occasions, while keeping a social smile on her face throughout.

Her cousin was, in fact, quite angry by the time the dance came to an end, although he tried not to show it.

'Dancing, it seems, sweet cousin, is not really your forte! As I know you are anxious to rejoin her, I will escort you back to the formidable Celestine now, but be assured, ma chere, I have already obtained Pierre's permission to take you into supper! So no little games, eh?'

Anna made no reply. After all, there was really very little she could say. If her grandfather had given Julien permission to escort her to supper, then she would have to let him do so, irksome as the prospect was.

As she sat down next to her grand-mother, Anna seized the opportunity of looking around the room.

Where was Patrick? So far, she hadn't seen anyone who remotely resembled him. Had he been invited to the ball? Surely he would have to have been as, at least ostensibly, a friend of Julien's . . .

Against her better judgement, she decided to ask Celestine.

'Grandmere, do you know if Patrick St Clair is here?'

'Does it matter to you that much?' Celestine asked, sadly. 'No don't answer that. I can tell from your face that it does. Very well then, he received an invitation, but, to my knowledge, he has not come. And it is almost ten o'clock. Supper will soon be served, so it hardly seems likely that he will come now, does it, Anna?'

Anna tried to tell herself that she didn't care, but, in actuality, she felt as if her heart was breaking . . .

Forcing a bright smile, she turned to her grandmother. And then her smile froze into a look of horror, as suddenly, bricks started to cascade through the ballroom windows, the sound of splintering glass echoing eerily with the music . . .

'Grandmere, what is happening?' Anna asked, her mouth dry with fear.

Celestine was as pale as a ghost.

'Oh God, it is them!' she cried, and Anna followed her gaze.

A horde of fierce-looking men were pouring into the room, through the broken windows, through the shattered door. They were brandishing knives and other weapons, and resembled creatures from some dark underworld.

'The Dubois!' Anna cried, knowing instinctively that this was who it must be.

Then she had no time for further coherent thought, as one of the ruffians grabbed hold of her, pulling her from her chair and holding her in front of himself like a shield, as he headed towards the door . . .

'Come on, Aristo, keep moving, or you'll feel this between your fine ribs!'

Anna was quaking with fear, aware that he was holding a knife to her back . . .

She couldn't take in anything else

that was happening in the room, although she was aware that it was in total chaos, people dashing this way and that, in a frantic effort to escape from the Dubois.

Then, suddenly, the knife's pressure was removed from her back, and she found herself being grasped hold of by a man in a raffish pirate's outfit.

'Quickly!' he mouthed at her. 'We have to get out of here!'

Acting on pure instinct, Anna allowed the pirate to hustle her from the room.

Once in the grounds, he took her hand, and pulled her towards the tables.

'I can't go so fast!' Anna protested, and, without a moment's hesitation, he swept her up into her arms.

'We'll be quicker this way,' he murmured, against her hair. And, as Anna had already suspected, she now realised without the trace of a doubt, that her rescuer was Patrick St Clair.

'Patrick!' she exclaimed. 'But I didn't

see you at the ball, didn't realise that you were there!'

'I was late arriving, sweetheart! I won't talk now, it's too important for us to make speed and get away from here, but I'll explain when we ride back to my house. All right?'

'Oh yes, Patrick! Thank God you arrived when you did!'

10

They mounted Cesar, whom Patrick had left tethered just inside the stable, and sped off in the direction of Patrick's manor house.

Anna was very conscious of his warm body in front of her on the horse, and it made her feel secure, although she was desperately worried about what must be happening at the chateau.

Patrick interrupted her troubled thoughts.

'I was late arriving at the ball because I had an unexpected visitor,' he explained. 'I'm sorry, I meant to be there much earlier, but it was necessary for me to . . . attend to this man first.

'Then, after I'd left Cesar in the stables, I noticed several ruffians hiding in the chateau grounds, and suspected that something of the sort was afoot.

After that, I just made all speed for the ballroom, knowing that I had to get you out of there as quickly as possible!'

'Didn't the Dubois see you, then? Otherwise, surely you would have been attacked and killed.' Anna shuddered, the thought of Patrick's death making her feel physically ill.

'I'm sure they did.' He smiled fleetingly in the darkness. 'But where the Dubois are concerned, I have to confess that I have a charmed life. I once saved one of their ringleaders' wives when she was in childbed. In return, he swore that I, and my property, would be spared from their attacks.'

'Oh, I see. Well, I suppose that's something! Oh, but Patrick, what will have become of my grandparents? Will the Dubois . . . kill them?' Anna's voice choked on the words. She might not see eye to eye with her grandparents, but she certainly didn't want to see them dead . . .

'I honestly don't know what they'll

do, Anna! I don't think they'll resort to something as drastic as murder. I think their intention is probably to frighten the landed gentry so much that they'll be prepared to listen to their grievances, although they're going about it in entirely the wrong way. Nevertheless, once I see that you're comfortably settled at my house, I will go back to the chateau and see what's happening.'

'You'll have to take care!' Anna exclaimed, in a frightened voice.

'You've no need to worry, ma cherie. As I told you, the Dubois have given their oath not to harm me!'

'And can you trust such as they?' Anna wanted to know.

'In their own way, they have a sort of loyalty, so I believe that I can,' Patrick replied.

By this time, they were pulling out the driveway of his home, and Anna saw Patrick's manor clearly for the first time, illuminated by the bright moonlight.

She had to admit that the sixteenth century dwelling looked much more comfortable than the fine, but austere lines of the de la Vigne chateau.

Patrick helped Anna to dismount, and gave Cesar's reins to a groom.

Then he rang the knocker, and a servant quickly opened the door.

'Why, Monsieur Patrick!' the woman exclaimed. 'You're back early! No trouble, I trust?'

'Later, Edith,' Patrick replied. 'I'll explain everything later! In the meantime, will you arrange that the Rose bed-chamber is made ready for my guest. She will be staying with us for a while.'

'Very good, sir,' Edith replied, with a curious glance at Anna before she hurried off to do her master's bidding.

'And now, Anna, ma cherie, if you're not too tired and distressed, I have someone here whom I think you will want to see.'

'You are referring to your visitor, I take it. But why should I want to see him? Surely I do not know him?'

Patrick slipped an arm around Ann's shoulders.

'You know him very well, Anna. My visitor is your father, who did not die in a duel as we supposed, although he was injured, and his journey here has reopened the wound.'

The colour drained from Anna's face, and she swayed slightly.

'Monsieur, if that is a joke, then it is in very poor taste!'

'I wouldn't dream of jesting about so serious a matter at a time like this!' Patrick replied in a stern voice, and Anna felt guilty for doubting him.

'Come, I will show you to the chamber where he lies abed, but be gentle with him. He has lost much blood and is quite weak.'

As if in a trance, Anna followed Patrick up the fine, oak staircase and to a room on the left-hand side.

Patrick tapped on the door, and a voice bade him enter. It was her father's voice, even if it was low, and sounded tired.

'Patrick, the shock of seeing me will not be too much for him?' Anna whispered, as Patrick opened the door.

'No, cherie, I assure you it won't. You see your father knows that Julien took you to France, which is why he came here looking for you.

'He stopped at my house because someone told him that I was a doctor, and his wound was troubling him sorely, due to the long journey.' He took Anna's hand, and led her into the dimly lit, but warm, and comfortable room.

'Henry, I have brought your daughter to see you.' And then he let go of Anna's hand. 'Stay with him or a few minutes. I will wait for you outside.'

Anna rushed forward to the bed, and bending down, dropped a kiss on her father's pale cheek. His hand came up and stroked her hair, and he looked at her with guilt in his green eyes, so very like her own.

'Oh Anna, my precious child! Can you forgive me for what I've done to you?'

'Of course I can!' Tears were glistening in Anna's eyes, and she brushed them away impatiently. 'I'm just so very, very happy to see that you're alive!'

Although she would have liked to, Anna knew better than to stay talking to her father for too long. He was obviously very weak, and needed sleep. They would, after all, have plenty of time to talk later.

When she went back out to join Patrick, her eyes were still glittering with tears.

'It was an emotional reunion, then?' he enquired, softly.

Anna nodded, still choked with tears of happiness.

'You must be feeling very tired, Anna, after all you've had more than your fair share of surprises for one day. Come, I'll escort you to the Rose room, and you can get some sleep.'

He opened the door of the room, and turned on the lamp.

It was a lovely, feminine room in soft shades of pink.

'I trust that it meets with your approval?'

'It's lovely,' she said, truthfully. 'Oh, Patrick! Why are you being so kind to me?'

Patrick made no answer, but, instead, drew her into the warm circle of his arms, his lips finding, and claiming, hers. A moment or two later he reluctantly drew away.

'There now, Anna, does that answer your question?'

The news from the chateau was bad.

Apparently, the whole place was in complete and utter chaos, with Pierre and Julien, along with a number of the other noblemen, going off in pursuit of the fleeing Dubois.

Worse was to follow. While no-one had actually been killed in the attack, Celestine had succumbed to a fatal heart attack.

'Then they killed her!' Anna had cried, distraught, when Patrick told her.

'They hastened her death, yes,' Patrick replied, sadly. 'But, if it is of any consolation, Anna, your grandmother could have died at any time, her heart was so bad. For certain, she would not have survived until summer, and she knew it.'

Anna looked up at him with accusing eyes.

'But why did you not tell me? After all, you must have known, seeing as you are a doctor!'

'She swore me to silence as she didn't wish to worry you,' he replied, gravely. 'If I'd had my way, she would have stayed in her bedchamber, resting.' He shrugged helplessly. 'But you know what a determined woman your grandmother was, she refused to listen.'

Anna gave a wan smile through her tears.

'No, she certainly wouldn't have

obeyed you about something like that. Oh Patrick! It seems such a terrible waste! She was such a vibrant person!'

Patrick sat down beside her on the settee, and took her hand in his.

'I know, Anna, I know! Yet she wouldn't wish you to grieve for her, she just wasn't that sort of person. And you must take heart. After all, even if you have lost Celestine, you have your father back again.'

'Yes, and me!' cried a raucous voice from the doorway, and the next moment Meg was in the room, and Anna was in her arms . . .

'Oh Meg, it's good to see you! You suffered no injury in the attack on the chateau?' Anna held her friend from Newgate at arm's length, and surveyed her anxiously.

Meg laughed.

'Of course not! Why would the rabble bother with the likes of me when I'm one of them!'

The following day, Pierre de la Vigne

returned to the chateau to make arrangements for his late wife's funeral. Julien, however, had declined returning with him, having decided that his place was in Paris.

'Your grandfather was very disappointed with him,' Patrick relayed to Anna later. 'He'd thought that at the very least Julien should have had the decency to remain for your grandmother's funeral.

'But, apparently, Julien told him that he had no further place at the chateau, that he wanted to live in the de la Vigne's Paris home, and that he was going to take up a career in politics.' Patrick smiled ruefully.

'Apparently, your cousin believes that he would make an excellent adviser to King Louis, whom, he declared, was 'Surrounded by liberal-minded fools!' All I can say, is God help poor France, should Julien succeed in influencing poor Louis!'

Despite herself, Anna smiled, picturing her arrogant cousin at the French king's court. Well, it was nice to know that Julien had decided to abandon his pursuit of her in favour of a political career!

She had known that Julien had never been in love with her. In fact, she very much doubted that he even liked her, but Pierre must feel doubly betrayed . . .

'I must go and see Grandpere,' she announced.

Patrick nodded.

'I'm sure he would like that. The funeral is to be held the day after tomorrow, so I suggest that we go and visit him tomorrow, that is, if you will allow me to accompany you?'

'I'd be happy for you to do so, Patrick, but, if you don't mind, I would speak to my grandfather alone.'

Patrick looked momentarily hurt.

'I know that perhaps now is not the right time to mention it, but I was hoping that I might speak to your grandfather in order to ask for your hand in marriage.'

Anna's breath caught in her throat, and she looked at him wordlessly, her love for him evident in her eyes.

'I've taken the liberty of speaking to your father, and he sees no handicap. In fact, he has accepted an offer of mine to stay on here at the manor and look after it for me. In turn, your Meg will look after him. They seem to have struck up something of a rapport. She's nursing him back to health — and probably not doing too good a job of it — she makes him laugh so much that I'm frightened his stitches will break!

'Anyway, she has accepted my offer of housekeeper here. I think between the two of them, they'll do a very good job of keeping the property safe!'

'Yes, I don't doubt it!' Anna agreed, with a smile. 'But will they be safe? What I mean to say is, you seem to consider that France could well be heading for a revolution!'

'Henry's an Englishmen, and Meg is 'one of them', so to speak. Also, as I explained to you earlier, I have a pledge from the Dubois not to harm my property.

'Of course, should they ever seem to be in the slightest danger, then they will always be welcome at my London home. But enough of them! What of you, Anna? Can I hope that you might do me the honour of becoming my wife?'

'Oh Patrick! I would that it was possible! But how can it be? You have been kind enough to provide for my father, but it doesn't change the fact that without you, both he and I are penniless! I would not wish to be a liability to you!'

'Anna, you could never be that!' Patrick exclaimed, vehemently. 'I am not a poor man, I have sufficient money for all of us!'

But Anna shook her head sadly.

'It just doesn't seem the same, though. I would constantly be afraid that you would grow to despise me, and that is something that I just couldn't stand!'

Patrick did his best to change Anna's mind, and, in the end, she compromised by agreeing to speak to her grandfather the following day and find out what his opinions on the matter were. After all, she owed the de la Vignes some loyalty . . .

Anna was glad that Patrick was accompanying her, as they travelled the short distance to the chateau, for she found that she was feeling quite nervous, her grandfather having expressed to Patrick his view that it was 'unseemly' for Anna to still be under his roof.

It was a bleak, wet day, and Patrick had instructed his coachman to bring out the carriage, so they arrived at the chateau in some style.

They didn't go near the shattered remnants of the ballroom, the sad events of a few days previously still too fresh in their minds for them to do so.

A servant let them in, and Patrick was shown into the petit salon, and served with coffee and cakes, while Anna was taken to her grandfather's study right away.

Pierre was seated behind his desk, just as he had been when Anna had first met him.

He stood up as she entered, and coming forward, took her into his arms and kissed her on both cheeks, in the French manner.

It was a better welcome than she had expected, and Anna's heart slowed from its former frantic beating.

'My dear child!' Pierre exclaimed, tears in his eyes. 'It is good to see you!'

'Grandpere, I am so very, very sorry about Grandmere. She was a wonderful person!' Anna exclaimed, and knew that she meant it. Celestine had been intimidating, but, for all that, she knew that she had been becoming increasingly fond of her grandmother . . .

'She was indeed,' Pierre agreed. 'For all our ups and downs, I know that I shall miss her terribly. But, thank the good Lord, I have been reunited with my dear granddaughter! Child, when are you coming back home?'

Anna felt her mouth go dry. She didn't know what to say!

'Well, I . . . I . . . Oh, Grandpere! I know that is perhaps not the time to speak of it, but I have received a proposal of marriage, one which I would very much like to accept!' There, the die was cast. She'd spoken of her feelings aloud. But what would her grandfather think? Would he be very angry?

'Sit down, Anna, and tell me all about this proposal,' her grandfather said quietly.

Well, at least he hadn't made an angry outburst! But what would he say when he knew that the man whom she wished to marry was Patrick? Not good enough, apparently, for a de la Vigne granddaughter, and yet too good for the penniless Miss Anna Heatherington?

There was only one way to find

out. As he had suggested, she must tell him.

Pierre de la Vigne heard Anna out in silence, his face totally expressionless.

When she had finished, he still didn't speak, just continued to gaze at her, his face inscrutable.

At last, he cleared his throat, and said gruffly.

'You could do worse. Patrick St Clair is a fine man.'

'Then you're not angry, Grandpere?' Anna's voice held incredulity.

'No, I'm not angry. I admit that I had harboured thoughts of you and Julien marrying, but I am beginning to see now that — that was just wishful thinking on my behalf, a desire for the de la Vigne name to continue, if you like! But I fear I have blinded myself to Julien's shortcomings, and, indeed, he has many.

'I have done a lot of thinking since that fateful night, and I see now that marriage to Julien would not have made you happy. Indeed, it could have proved tragic, for he is not a man to move with the times.

'Now, I think I have some news for you which will be pleasing. You tell me that, even if I give my permission, which is probably only a formality anyway, now that your father has reappeared from the grave, so to speak, that you still hesitate about marrying Patrick due to your financial position.

'Well, you need worry about that no longer, Anna, for your grandmother has left you her own considerable personal fortune — inherited from her late father, and kept in her own name due to a pre-nuptial agreement.'

Anna's face mirrored her amazement . . .

'But why would she do that?'

'Because, in the short time that she had known you, she had grown very fond of you, ma cherie, and she also wanted to make amends for her treatment of your mother, something which we both came to regret. Your grandmother informed me that she intended to change her will, and lawyers came to the chateau and saw to this in accordance with her wishes.

'The new will was secreted in her room, and is now in the hands of the lawyers. So you see, Anna, you are no penniless chit of a girl, but a noblewoman with a considerable fortune.' His dark eyes twinkled. 'So you can marry with a dowry. The only stipulation that I make is that you have a formal betrothal, and do not marry until a respectable interval of time has elapsed since your grandmother's death.' He gave a wistful smile.

'Even though your father is in residence, I am not sure that I quite approve of you living in your future bridegroom's home, so perhaps you would consider coming home to your grandpere during the period of your betrothal?'

Anna stood up and walked over to her grandfather, bent down, and kissed the weathered cheek.

'Grandpere, I would be very happy

to do so. And thank you, thank you so much!'

Patrick was pacing about in the petit salon, his coffee only half consumed, and the cakes untouched.

He turned, throwing a worried look in Anna's direction, as she opened the door and ran in, not having even paused to knock.

'What news?' he asked, a muscle at the side of his mouth betraying his inner turmoil.

Anna threw herself into his arms.

'The answer's yes, Patrick. Yes, yes, yes!' And she went on to explain about Celestine leaving her personal fortune to Anna.

But Patrick wasn't even listening, as he visualised a lifetime of happiness with the woman he loved.

Other titles in the Linford Romance Library

SAVAGE PARADISE
Sheila Belshaw

For four years, Diana Hamilton had dreamed of returning to Luangwa Valley in Zambia. Now she was back — and, after a close encounter with a rhino — was receiving a lecture from a tall, khaki-clad man on the dangers of going into the bush alone!

PAST BETRAYALS
Giulia Gray

As soon as Jon realized that Julia had fallen in love with him, he broke off their relationship and returned to work in the Middle East. When Jon's best friend, Danny, proposed a marriage of friendship, Julia accepted. Then Jon returned and Julia discovered her love for him remained unchanged.

PRETTY MAIDS ALL IN A ROW
Rose Meadows

The six beautiful daughters of George III of England dreamt of handsome princes coming to claim them, but the King always found some excuse to reject proposals of marriage. This is the story of what befell the Princesses as they began to seek lovers at their father's court, leaving behind rumours of secret marriages and illegitimate children.

THE GOLDEN GIRL
Paula Lindsay

Sarah had everything — wealth, social background, great beauty and magnetic charm. Her heart was ruled by love and compassion for the less fortunate in life. Yet, when one man's happiness was at stake, she failed him — and herself.

A DREAM OF HER OWN
Barbara Best

A stranger gently kisses Sarah Danbury at her Betrothal Ball. Little does she realise that she is to meet this mysterious man again in very different circumstances.

HOSTAGE OF LOVE
Nara Lake

From the moment pretty Emma Tregear, the only child of a Van Diemen's Land magnate, met Philip Despard, she was desperately in love. Unfortunately, handsome Philip was a convict on parole.

THE ROAD TO BENDOUR
Joyce Eaglestone

Mary Mackenzie had lived a sheltered life on the family farm in Scotland. When she took a job in the city she was soon in a romantic maze from which only she could find the way out.

NEW BEGINNINGS
Ann Jennings

On the plane to his new job in a hospital in Turkey, Felix asked Harriet to put their engagement on hold, as Philippe Krir, the Director of Bodrum hospital, refused to hire 'attached' people. But, without an engagement ring, what possible excuse did Harriet have for holding Philippe at bay?

THE CAPTAIN'S LADY
Rachelle Edwards

1820: When Lianne Vernon becomes governess at Elswick Manor, she finds her young pupil is given to strange imaginings and that her employer, Captain Gideon Lang, is the most enigmatic man she has ever encountered. Soon Lianne begins to fear for her pupil's safety.

THE VAUGHAN PRIDE
Margaret Miles

As the new owner of Southwood Manor, Laura Vaughan discovers that she's even more poverty stricken than before. She also finds that her neighbour, the handsome Marius Kerr, is a little too close for comfort.

HONEY-POT
Mira Stables

Lovely, well-born, well-dowered, Russet Ingram drew all men to her. Yet here she was, a prisoner of the one man immune to her graces — accused of frivolously tampering with his young ward's romance!

DREAM OF LOVE
Helen McCabe

When there is a break-in at the art gallery she runs, Jade can't believe that Corin Bossinney is a trickster, or that she'd fallen for the oldest trick in the book . . .

FOR LOVE OF OLIVER
Diney Delancey

When Oliver Scott buys her family home, Carly retains the stable block from which she runs her riding school. But she soon discovers Oliver is not an easy neighbour to have. Then Carly is presented with a new challenge, one she must face for love of Oliver.

THE SECRET OF MONKS' HOUSE
Rachelle Edwards

Soon after her arrival at Monks' House, Lilith had been told that it was haunted by a monk, and she had laughed. Of greater interest was their neighbour, the mysterious Fabian Delamaye. Was he truly as debauched as rumour told, and what was the truth about his wife's death?

THE SPANISH HOUSE
Nancy John

Lynn couldn't help falling in love with the arrogant Brett Sackville. But Brett refused to believe that she felt nothing for his half-brother, Rafael. Lynn knew that the cruel game Brett made her play to protect Rafael's heart could end only by breaking hers.

N

PROUD SURGEON
Lynne Collins

Calder Savage, the new Senior Surgical Officer at St. Antony's Hospital, had really lived up to his name, venting a savage irony on anyone who fell foul of him. But when he gave Staff Nurse Honor Portland a lift home, she was surprised to find what an interesting man he was.